Praise for the Adventures of Lily Lapp series

"A simple look at Amish life through the eye of a child; great book for a group or family read; short chapters to hold little ones' attentions; easy to read for ages 8–12; entertaining."

—*Christian Manifesto*

"This is truly a gem. Similar to the Little House on the Prairie stories, we learn about the Amish way of life and get to meet several of Lily's family's friends and relatives. This is an excellent book for young readers; it offers a different perspective and point of view while still entertaining."

—*Fiction Addict*

"Adults' concerns about making ends meet, illness, and death lap at Lily's life, but her parents prove an unbreachable levee, protecting her and their way of life. The simple prose focused on daily living will appeal to those who like realistic fiction."

—*Publishers Weekly*

"Lily enjoys the adventures of each new day. As you travel with her, you'll learn the Amish way of life. The humor and wonderment of childhood is worth the read."

—*RT Book Reviews*

A Surprise *for* Lily

Books by Suzanne Woods Fisher
and Mary Ann Kinsinger

THE ADVENTURES OF LILY LAPP

Life with Lily

A New Home for Lily

A Big Year for Lily

A Surprise for Lily

Books by Suzanne Woods Fisher

Amish Peace: Simple Wisdom for a Complicated World

Amish Proverbs: Words of Wisdom from the Simple Life

*Amish Values for Your Family: What We Can Learn from the
Simple Life*

LANCASTER COUNTY SECRETS

The Choice

The Waiting

The Search

A Lancaster County Christmas

SEASONS OF STONEY RIDGE

The Keeper

The Haven

The Lesson

THE ADVENTURES OF LILY LAPP

Book Four

A Surprise *for* Lily

Mary Ann Kinsinger and Suzanne Woods Fisher

Revell
a division of Baker Publishing Group
Grand Rapids, Michigan

© 2013 by Suzanne Woods Fisher and Mary Ann Kinsinger

Published by Revell
a division of Baker Publishing Group
P.O. Box 6287, Grand Rapids, MI 49516-6287
www.revellbooks.com

Printed in the United States of America

Library of Congress Cataloging-in-Publication Data
Kinsinger, Mary Ann.
    A surprise for Lily / Mary Ann Kinsinger and Suzanne Woods Fisher.
        pages cm. — (The adventures of Lily Lapp ; book 4)
    Summary: Lily Lapp, now in fifth grade and growing up fast, faces many changes including old friends leaving and new ones coming, the election of a new bishop, and a wedding. Includes facts about the Amish faith and way of life.
    ISBN 978-0-8007-2135-0 (pbk.)
    1. Amish—Juvenile fiction. [1. Amish—Fiction. 2. Family life—Pennsylvania—Fiction. 3. Friendship—Fiction. 4. Schools—Fiction. 5. Pennsylvania—Fiction.] I. Fisher, Suzanne Woods. II. Title.
PZ7.K62933Sur 2013
[Fic]—dc23   2013017654

Scripture quotations, whether quoted or paraphrased, are from the King James Version of the Bible.

Published in association with Joyce Hart of The Hartline Literary Agency, LLC

13   14   15   16   17   18   19   7   6   5   4   3   2   1

Contents

Contents

Lily's First
and Last Rowboat Trip

All morning, Lily hurried to pull weeds in the garden. As soon as she finished, Mama said, she could spend the rest of the day at Cousin Hannah's house. After Lily had worked so hard in the hot August sun, only to rush over to Hannah's house, she arrived to disappointment. Hannah was helping her mother can peaches in a steamy kitchen. Next to weeding the garden on a hot summer day, Lily's least favorite job was to can fruit.

One by one, Aunt Mary halved the peaches and Hannah and Lily dropped the peaches into clean glass jars. When the last jar was filled, the girls washed their sticky hands under the faucet, happy to be free to spend the rest of the day outdoors.

Hannah grabbed a loaf of bread from the shelf in the pantry. "Let's feed the fish in our pond."

"Does your mother mind if we use that bread?" Lily asked.

"Nope," Hannah said. "We always feed stale bread to the fish. This bread was baked yesterday, so it isn't fresh any longer."

The bread was stale after just one day? That wasn't Mama's way of thinking. But Lily wanted to help Hannah feed the fish so she didn't say another word about it. No indeed! Not one word.

"We have a surprise by the pond," Hannah said as they hurried down the dirt path that led through the pasture to the pond.

"Will I like it?" Lily asked. Hannah was much more bold and adventurous than she was. It wouldn't surprise her if Hannah had something horrible and frightening to show her, like an ugly bullfrog or a snake with pointy fangs.

Hannah skipped along. "Oh, you'll like it a lot."

When the girls reached the pond, Lily spotted an old, worn-out green rowboat along the shoreline. "A boat?"

"Yes! My dad bought it last week and gives us rides in it every evening. I can even help row it."

"Why is it upside down?"

"Dad flips it upside down each night so no water can get inside if it rains," Hannah said. "Help me turn it over so you can see what it looks like on the inside."

Lily bent down to help Hannah lift the rowboat. It was heavier than it looked. They lifted as hard as they could. Lily was afraid it might slip and come crashing down right on top of their fingers. With one final grunt and an extra hard shove, they managed to push the boat upright so that it toppled over. The girls puffed and panted, impressed with their own strength.

The interior of the boat had two smoothly varnished bench seats. Hannah climbed in. "Let's sit inside to feed the fish."

Lily scrambled into the boat to join her. They broke off bits of bread from the loaf. Now and then, if they watched carefully as they tossed a piece of bread into the water, a fish would snap the bait and the bread would disappear, leaving only bubbles behind. Dragonflies skated over the surface of the still water.

"Do you see the water lilies growing on the other side of the pond? I helped my dad plant them this spring." Hannah sighed. "I don't think I'll see them when they grow big and tall."

Lily tossed a piece of bread out farther. "Why not?"

Hannah lowered her voice to a whisper. "I think we're going to move."

Lily froze. It felt as if she had just been hit by a rock and was in that in-between moment before it hurt so terribly. "Why?" she asked. "But why? I thought your family was happy here."

"I like it here just fine," Hannah said. "But Levi and I have been eavesdropping on Mama and Papa. We've heard them say things like, 'It didn't take the children long to make new friends here, so they shouldn't have any problem making new friends again.'"

It couldn't be true! It just couldn't. Surely, Lily's parents would have heard about it. After all, Mama and Aunt Mary were sisters. Hannah must have misheard. She was known for mixing things up and starting rumors based on her mix-ups. Hannah had a flair for the dramatic.

Lily couldn't bear to think of Hannah moving away. So she did what she always did when she didn't want to think about something. She changed the subject. "It would be fun to feed the fish out in the middle of the pond."

13

"We could row the boat out there," Hannah said.

Lily hesitated. "I've never rowed a boat."

"Oh, it's a snap!" Hannah said, snapping her fingers to show Lily just how easy it was. "I could teach you." She tossed the loaf of bread into the bottom of the boat and hopped out. "Help me push the boat into the water."

The two girls pushed and shoved, pushed and shoved. The bottom of the boat scraped over stones and dirt to the edge of the pond. Hannah held the boat steady and told Lily to get in.

Lily climbed over the side and sat down quickly. The rocking motion made her feel as if she might pitch right over the side. Hannah scrambled in, tipping the boat wildly while Lily clutched her seat. Then she unclipped the oars from the side of the boat and handed one to Lily. Hannah jammed an oar into the bank to push off. She fit each oar through a lock, a steel hook, on each side of the boat. "Just watch and do what I do."

The oar felt heavy and clumsy in Lily's hands as she tried to dip it into the water to paddle. It was much harder than it looked. The boat drifted out toward the middle of the pond as Lily tried to help Hannah row. Instead of going in a nice straight line they kept going around and around in circles. It wasn't long before Hannah grew impatient with Lily's feeble rowing. "You need to dip your oar deeper into the water to paddle." She rowed harder to show Lily exactly what she meant, pulling the water with hardly a ripple.

"I can't do it exactly like you're doing," Lily said. Her frustration built, minute by minute. "You couldn't paddle very well either if you were sitting on this side of the boat."

"Oh, yes I could," Hannah said. "Let's trade places and I'll show you." She got up to move to Lily's side of the boat.

The boat rocked and Lily quickly gripped her seat with both hands to steady herself.

"Oh no! Why did you do that?"

Lily looked up at her in surprise. "Do what? What did I do?"

"The oar! You've dropped the oar into the water."

Lily felt her mouth drop open. She had been so concerned about the boat tipping over that she had let go of the oar! It was floating away from the boat.

"We have to get it so we can row back to the shore," Hannah said.

The girls leaned over the side of the boat to try to reach the oar, but it was just beyond their reach. They stretched a little farther, then a little bit more. Then Lily got the scare of her life. The boat tilted so far that the girls spilled headfirst into the water.

Lily couldn't swim! She kicked and flailed, panicking, sure she was going to drown. Her head popped up out of the water and she coughed. One hand brushed the side of the boat, and she managed to grab it and hang on. Hannah had grabbed the boat, too. Her eyes were wide with fright as she looked at Lily.

"How do we get back in?" Lily asked, struggling to hold on to the slippery boat.

"I don't think we can," Hannah said.

"Then there's only one thing we can do," Lily said. "Help!"

Hannah chimed in. "Help! Help!" Over and over they called out, but the pond was quite a distance from the house. Most likely, Aunt Mary couldn't even hear them calling, and Levi was helping Uncle Elmer build mini barns. The machinery was probably making too much noise for them to hear the girls' cries for help. Lily's arms grew tired from hanging on to the side of the boat and her voice was getting hoarse from yelling so much. She wished she had never stepped foot in that boat.

Just when Lily was sure she and Hannah would drown, Aunt Mary came running. "Hang on to the boat!" she called from the pond's edge. "I'll get help." She turned and ran to get Uncle Elmer from the barn.

The sight of Uncle Elmer running toward the pond, as fast as he could, was one of the best visions Lily had ever seen. They weren't going to die after all! He didn't even stop to remove his shoes when he got to the edge of the water. He jumped right in and swam out to the middle of the pond. He helped them climb into the boat and then started swimming slowly back to the shore, pushing the boat as he swam.

Once Hannah and Lily were safely on the bank, Uncle

Elmer dragged himself out of the pond and lay in the grass, panting and coughing. Aunt Mary put a hand on each of the girls' shoulders and marched them back to the house. "I thought you knew better than to go out on that boat by yourself," she said to Hannah.

"It's my fault," Lily said quietly. "I thought it would be fun to feed the fish from the middle of the pond."

Aunt Mary didn't say anything else to the girls other than to send them upstairs to Hannah's room to change into dry clothes.

As soon as Lily was in a dry dress borrowed from Hannah, she decided to go home. This afternoon hadn't turned out very well.

Aunt Mary stopped her at the door and handed her a note. "Give this to your mother when you get home."

Oh no. Not a *note*! Why did grown-ups always feel the need to inform each other of their children's misdeeds? Why couldn't some things be left unsaid? Lily slipped the note into her dress pocket and trudged home. It wasn't the best day of her life.

Mama had a curious look on her face when she saw Lily come into the house with Hannah's dress on. "Did something happen today?"

"I . . . might have . . . fallen . . . into the pond," Lily said. She handed Aunt Mary's note to Mama and saw a look of concern sweep over her.

"Oh Lily," Mama said, "you could have drowned! Why would you go out in a pond when you don't even know how to swim?" She clapped her hands to her cheeks.

"When are you going to learn to stop and think about what could happen *before* you get yourself into trouble?"

But it wasn't easy to anticipate every disaster. Mama made it sound so simple, but it was so much easier for Lily to know what things she shouldn't have done after she had done them.

Mama shook her head, exasperated. "Change your clothes before you get Hannah's dress dirty or torn."

Lily went up to her bedroom to change her clothes, then stopped abruptly on the top step. In the terror of nearly drowning, she had completely forgotten the other terrible news. Hannah might be moving away! The thought of saying goodbye to Hannah was the next worst thing to drowning that could happen to Lily. She galloped down the stairs and burst into the kitchen. "Mama! Is Hannah moving away?"

Mama looked up from the stove, startled. It took her a moment to answer. She took the pot off the burner and set it on the back of the stove. Then she crossed the room to Lily and sat in a chair, pointing out the chair next to her for Lily to use. As Lily sat, a terrible feeling started in her stomach. "Yes. Aunt Mary and Uncle Elmer want to move."

Lily tried to blink back the tears that were stinging her eyes. "But why?"

"Uncle Elmer's father is retiring from farming. He asked them to come live on their farm."

There was no stopping Lily's tears now. They spilled down her cheeks, one after the other. "When?" she asked, barely a whisper. "When will Hannah move away?"

"As soon as their farm sells," Mama said gently. She brushed the tears off Lily's cheeks. "Don't cry. Life is full of changes. Even if we feel sad that they'll be moving away, we know it's the right thing for them to do. And you and Hannah can always write letters to each other. Once a year, we'll be sure to visit them."

Once a year didn't sound nearly often enough to see Cousin Hannah. She was just about to say so to Mama, but then she noticed that Mama's eyes looked bright and shiny, as if she might be trying not to cry. It dawned on Lily that she had been thinking only about how much she would miss Hannah. Aunt Mary was Mama's sister. "Don't worry, Mama," Lily said, patting her shoulder. "Maybe their farm will take a long time to sell."

"Maybe so." Mama gave her a shaky smile before she rose and went back to the stove.

Lily was still upset, but she tried to put on a brave front. For Mama's sake.

The Disappearing Garden Boot

Mama went out to the garden before breakfast to pick some green beans. When she came back inside, she had an exasperated look on her face. As the family gathered to sit at the table, Mama asked, "Does anyone know where one of my gardening boots went?" She set a platter of scrambled eggs in front of Papa. "Last evening, I set both of them next to each other on the front porch when I finished up in the garden. This morning, I can only find one boot."

But no one had any idea where Mama's boot was. After breakfast, Lily, Joseph, and Dannie searched high and low for the boot. It was nowhere to be seen. It had vanished into thin air.

"I hope it turns up soon," Mama said. "I don't mind working in the garden in my bare feet, but it's a different story for the sweet corn patch. Too many rocks in it."

And snakes, Lily thought. *Don't forget about snakes.*

⁖⧽×⧼⁖

Several days later, Lily spent most of the afternoon writing a circle letter to her same-aged girl cousins. She held it up for one more admiring read-through before she folded it and stuck it in the envelope. Her cursive handwriting was excellent. Just excellent. It was too bad there wasn't a school prize for the student with the Most Excellent Cursive. She would surely win it and wouldn't that make Effie Kauffman mad? Lily smiled at the thought.

Dear cousins,

Greetings of love sent to you all. Hope my scribbles find you all healthy and happy. We are all doing fine.

Last week was our in-between Sunday. Mama and I packed a picnic lunch of sandwiches, fresh cherries, and popcorn. Then we went on a drive in the spring wagon. Papa wants to build more seats for it someday but for now we made little blanket nests in the back to sit in.

Joseph, Dannie, and I had fun seeing who could spit cherry stones the farthest while Papa drove the wagon. Paul is still too little to spit stones so Mama had to take the stones out of his cherries for him.

Papa drove along some new roads. It's always fun to see where we end up. At one place there was water coming out of the side of the hill beside the road. Papa stopped to give Jim a drink. We all took a turn getting a drink. It was very cold.

Joseph, Dannie, and I have been busy picking potato bugs in the garden. We get a nickel for every dozen we pick. I don't like touching them so I use a twig to scrape them off the leaves and into an empty can. Joseph and Dannie don't mind touching them, but you know boys.

It's dry here. We all hope it rains soon. It's hard work to water everything in the garden. Papa carries five-gallon pails with water to the edge of the garden and then Joseph, Dannie, and I water the plants with it.

There is a frog living under some of our tomato plants. It hopped out on my toes once, and I screamed so loud that Papa came running out of his shop. I don't like frogs, but Mama says it eats bugs. I wish it would eat the potato bugs.

Only a few more weeks until school starts for the new term. We're going to have a new teacher this year. I haven't met her yet because she's from another district. But I do know her name: Teacher Judith. Isn't that a pretty name? I can hardly wait for fifth grade to start!

Love,
Lily

Satisfied, Lily ran to the mailbox to put the letter in it before the mailman came by. Sitting under the mailbox was the biggest dog she had ever seen. In its mouth was Mama's lone boot. She turned right around and ran to the house, shouting for Mama. "Come quick! Your other boot. There's a dog chewing on it!"

The dog followed Lily all the way to the house and sat on the porch as if he'd been invited for tea and cake. Joseph

tried to shoo it away. The dog leaped down the porch steps, Mama's boot still in its mouth.

"Hey!" Joseph yelled. "Come back here!" He ran after the dog to try to get Mama's boot back. The dog turned to see what the ruckus was all about. Just as Joseph got close to him, the dog ran off. It was funny to watch. The dog would stop and turn, daring Joseph to catch him. Just as Joseph drew close and nearly caught him, off he would run again. Over and over, that dog teased Joseph.

Lily and Mama watched from the porch. "Lily, you'd better go with Joseph and help him get the boot back."

Lily ran after Joseph, who ran after the dog. Down the

driveway, across the road, and into the woods. As soon as Joseph and Lily were almost near enough to grab the boot out of the dog's mouth, the dog would run off again. Deeper and deeper into the woods they ran. Gasping for air, Lily suggested it might be wise to give up and go home.

"Not yet," Joseph said, puffing and panting. "I'm sure we can catch him soon." So they kept going, crashing through underbrush and hopping over fallen branches.

Lily was hot and sweaty and worried they were too far from home. The big dog seemed to know exactly where he was going, trotting along a trail as if he had all the time in the world. Up ahead, the dog disappeared into an old abandoned train tunnel. Lily and Joseph stopped at the mouth of the tunnel, debating what to do.

Joseph, naturally, wanted to go exploring. "If the dog can go into it, so can we."

Lily wasn't convinced. The tunnel was long and dark and scary, and it smelled musty. But then a breeze of cool air floated out of the tunnel's entrance. It did feel good, that cool air. Joseph took a few steps into the tunnel. "Come on, Lily," he said. "I can see the other end of it. I see a patch of light ahead."

Hearing that there was an end to the tunnel was encouraging news. The last thing Lily wanted to do was to get lost in a dark tunnel and never be seen again. She took a few steps in, then a few more. And then she hurried to catch up with Joseph. The farther they walked, the darker the tunnel became. Water dripped from the ceiling, making spooky *plink plunk* noises as it landed on the dirt floor of the tunnel.

They kept walking until they were stopped by a large mound of dirt that had fallen from the roof of the tunnel. At this point, Lily's fears rose up again and she hesitated.

"What if more dirt falls on us?" More importantly, what if the ceiling caved in and they were buried alive?

"It won't," Joseph said, scrambling over the dirt. Lily followed him—what else could she do?—and they kept going toward the light at the other end of the tunnel. Finally, they reached the exit. The bright sunshine hurt their eyes. The big white dog lay under a tree, chewing on Mama's boot. He raised his head and looked at them as if to say, "What took you so long?"

Joseph ran off to catch the dog, and wouldn't you just know what happened next? That dog waited until Joseph reached out a hand to grab the boot and off he ran. Now Joseph was mad. He was all the more determined to get Mama's boot back.

Joseph followed the dog and Lily followed Joseph. They came to a clearing and spotted a little log cabin tucked against a grove of trees. The dog went up the porch steps of the log cabin and lay down at the feet of an old, old, old man. Lily thought he might be even older than Great-Grandma had been, and she'd been ancient. He had the longest, scraggliest beard she had ever seen, and she had seen a lot of beards in church. This old man's beard flowed down his chest, like a river of gray crinkles. It looked as if he had never had his hair cut. His white hair was braided and hung down his back. It touched the porch floor.

The old man noticed Lily and Joseph. "Ah, visitors," he said at last. "Rufus likes me to have company." He stroked the head of the big white dog.

Joseph spoke up first. He was always doing that, and it made Lily mad. "We followed your dog all the way here. He ran off with our mama's boot."

The old man laughed and slapped his hands on his knees. "So that's where he got the boot. The other day he brought a boot home and I put it in the woodshed. If you don't mind getting it, you can take the pair of them back to their rightful owner."

Joseph found the boot in the woodshed, just like the old man said. Lily stayed right where she was, watching everything. Just in case.

"Say, would you like to stay and eat with me?" the old man said. "I have some venison stew on the stove. There's plenty to share."

Joseph looked like he was just about to say yes, so Lily quickly intervened. "We need to get home," she said. "Papa and Mama might be worried about us."

The man nodded. "You tell your Papa and Mama to come for a visit, anytime. Tell them my name is Teaskoota, and I'm a Shawnee Indian. Might be the oldest man alive. It gets a little lonely up here, and Rufus ain't much for small talk."

Rufus was sprawled out on the porch, sound asleep.

Lily and Joseph started toward home. They each held one of Mama's boots. Before they left the clearing, Lily turned to look at everything again. It was like a picture in her history book: a log cabin, a little log barn. A small pasture with oxen in it, enclosed with a wooden split-rail fence. She wondered why anyone would live such a lonely, old-fashioned life.

"Come on, Lily," Joseph said.

Lily waved to Teaskoota and followed Joseph back into the woods, through the long dark tunnel, and along the dim trail. She was glad when she saw the sign for Whispering Pines. Papa and Mama looked relieved to see them come up the driveway. Papa said he was just about to go looking for them. Mama was delighted to see the boots in their hands.

When Lily and Joseph told them about Teaskoota and his log cabin, Papa nodded as if he knew all about him. "That's the man whom Aaron Yoder helped a few summers ago. Remember? Everyone thought Aaron was lost and spent days looking for him."

Lily remembered. She had often thought about that old man and had wished Aaron Yoder had just stayed with him. But now that she met Teaskoota and discovered how nice he was, how kind he was to them, and how happy he was to have company, she wouldn't wish Aaron Yoder on him. She wasn't heartless.

Finding Dozer

A little brown mother wren sat on the roof of the wooden birdhouse that hung in a tree near the clothesline. She chattered at Lily, warning her to stay away as if she had babies in the snug little birdhouse. It was August, and her wren babies were long gone.

Lily picked up the last wet shirt from the laundry basket and handed it to Mama to hang on the clothesline. As she started back to the laundry room in the basement, she turned the basket upside down to dump the excess water out. Rounding the corner of the house, she saw a dark green minivan pull into the driveway. She dropped the laundry basket and ran back to Mama. "We have visitors!" she said.

Mama wiped her hands on the sides of her apron and hurried over to see who had arrived. Lily was curious about the visitors, but shyness swooped in and she ducked through the basement door. She ran over to the shop where Papa was

working. He shut the sander off when he saw her by the door.
"Papa, we have visitors!"

Papa brushed the sawdust off his arms and shirt and went
outside. Lily stood inside the door and peeked out to see if she
knew who had come. She saw an Amish couple climb out of
the green minivan. Papa hurried over and shook hands with
the man, and then they both slapped each other's back. Why,
it was Papa's older brother, Uncle Ira!

Then Lily noticed a tall, gaunt woman standing next to
Mama. *Oh, boy.* Lily would never forget her: Aunt Tillie,
Uncle Ira's wife.

The driver of the minivan got out of the car to talk to Papa, then everyone started to walk toward the shop. Lily dashed back to the basement laundry room so they wouldn't catch her spying on them. She grabbed Mama's wooden stick and fished clothes out of the steaming hot water in the washing machine. Just as Mama and Aunt Tillie came into the basement, Lily tried to lift a wet shirt out and drop it into the clean rinse water.

"My goodness, Rachel, you already have a big girl," Aunt Tillie said. "She's in here doing the laundry all by herself."

Lily tried to hide her delight at Aunt Tillie's compliment but was not very successful. She didn't expect something nice and friendly from Aunt Tillie's mouth. She reminded Lily of a skinny version of Effie's mother, Ida Kauffman.

"Lily is a fine helper," Mama said, amused by Lily's giant grin. She took the wooden stick from Lily's hands and fished the clothes out of the hot soapy water of the washing machine to drop them into the tub filled with cold rinse water.

Aunt Tillie put down her things and pitched right in with the laundry. It didn't take long to finish rinsing and hanging the clothes on the line. And soon it was time to make lunch.

⚬⚬⚬

As everyone gathered for lunch, Uncle Ira introduced the driver of the minivan to Lily, Joseph, and Dannie as an English man named Bill. He was quite intrigued by Papa's woodshop and had spent most of the morning watching Papa work.

Bill took several bites of Mama's chunky potato salad. "Nice little business you have, Daniel," he said. He wiped his mouth with a napkin and repeated himself. "Really nice little business you have there."

Pleased, Papa said, "It helps put food on the table."

Aunt Tillie and Uncle Ira did the rest of the talking during lunch, catching up Mama and Papa on all the latest news with the Kentucky Lapp family. "Things have been awful dry in Kentucky this summer," Uncle Ira said. "Quite a few families are thinking of moving north to better farmland. Our married children already have their farms for sale and hope to move before winter."

Aunt Tillie made a sour face.

There was the Aunt Tillie whom Lily remembered from a visit to Kentucky years ago!

"It's a shame, that's what it is," Aunt Tillie said, tsk-tsking with her tongue. "It's so hard to have to start over in a new place when you're a young family without a lot of money. I'm trying to talk Ira into moving with them. That way, we'd be there to help them out if they need anything."

Uncle Ira concentrated on his lunch. He mopped the last bits of food from his plate with a piece of bread, almost as if he didn't even hear Aunt Tillie. But Lily had a hunch that once Aunt Tillie made her mind up about something, she would get her way.

As Mama cleared the plates, Papa said, "Since you'll be here for a few days, I thought it might be fun if we go to the rock bed tomorrow."

Lily sat up a little straighter in her chair. Papa had such good ideas. She had been to the rock bed only once in her life, soon after her family had moved to Cloverdale. Beth's parents had invited them to a picnic at the rock bed.

Aunt Tillie made yet another sour face. "What's a rock bed?"

"It's a small field in the middle of the woods," Papa said. "About the size of a school playground. It's covered completely with one huge rock that's been cracked in several different places. One edge of the rock bed is almost three feet high but most of it is much higher than that. You have to see it in order to be able to grasp how majestic it really is."

Uncle Ira's bushy eyebrows lifted. "That sounds interesting."

Aunt Tillie turned to Mama. "Rachel, what do you have planned for us to do while the men are out rock climbing?"

Papa and Mama exchanged a look. "I thought we could all go," Papa said.

"Oh no!" Aunt Tillie said. "You won't catch me clawing my way up over a pile of rocks."

Lily had to clap her hand over her mouth to keep down a giggle at the picture that came to mind: Aunt Tillie in her dark dress and stern face, clinging to the side of a rocky cliff with those long, bony fingers.

"We don't have to do any actual climbing, Tillie," Mama said. "I think you'll enjoy it." There was a firmness to Mama's voice that surprised Lily. She wondered if Mama didn't want to have to spend a day alone with Aunt Tillie. At least, that's what was on Lily's mind.

❦

Lily woke to the sweet smell of baked bread. Mama had gotten up extra early to bake rolls for today's picnic. After the breakfast dishes were washed, Lily helped Mama and Aunt Tillie prepare a picnic lunch. Lily shredded the leftover chicken from last night's supper, then mixed in the salad dressing Mama had scooped into a measuring cup. Mama added a few pinches of salt from the salt box. That was a mystery to Lily. How did Mama know the right amount of salt to add without measuring? Lily had to measure everything or she ended up with disasters. "Dis-as-tahs," Joseph called Lily's cooking mistakes.

After stirring the shredded chicken, chopped celery, and dressing, Lily spread it on Mama's fresh baked rolls. She could hardly wait for lunch. Chicken salad sandwiches would taste delicious on their picnic.

Aunt Tillie squeezed lemons for lemonade while Mama cleaned carrots and cucumbers from the garden. All that was left to pack were Mama's enormous chocolate chip cookies. By the time the picnic basket was filled and ready to go, Papa had hitched Jim to the spring wagon. He had placed blankets in the back for the children to sit on. Uncle Ira brought two kitchen chairs for Mama and Aunt Tillie.

The rock bed was ten miles away. It would take Jim at least two hours to get there. It was a heavy load for Jim to pull, and Lily was glad the sky was overcast and the air was cool. Papa worried about Jim. He stopped frequently to let Jim rest, which annoyed Aunt Tillie. "Seems like it's time you find yourself a new buggy horse, Daniel," she told him more than once.

Lily didn't like to hear Aunt Tillie talk about Jim as if he were just an old thing to be replaced. Jim was as much a part of their family as Dannie and Paul.

Lily tried to block out Aunt Tillie's whiny voice. She loved long drives in the fresh open air, and she couldn't stop thinking about those chicken sandwiches that would be waiting for them.

Lily and Joseph and Dannie played I Spy until Dannie fell asleep. Then Joseph fell asleep and Lily was left to play I Spy all by herself, which wasn't much fun.

At long last, they arrived at the rock bed. It looked just as big as she had remembered it. Papa tied Jim to a tree, then helped Mama and baby Paul out of the wagon. He put a slice of hay on the ground for Jim to enjoy while they had their picnic. He carried the picnic basket in one hand and Paul in the other as they walked to the edge of the rock. It towered above them. When they reached the edge that was only about three feet off the ground, Papa set the picnic basket down and handed Paul to Mama. Uncle Ira clambered up on the rock with a little push from Papa. Then Papa hoisted himself up. He reached down to help Lily, Joseph, and Dannie up. Then Mama handed Paul up to Papa, and he put him in Lily's arms. Then Papa helped Mama and Aunt Tillie up. Everyone looked all around the rock bed and Uncle Ira let out a long, low whistle. "I had no idea it would be like this." Even Aunt Tillie seemed impressed, which was something to behold. It wasn't easy to impress Aunt Tillie.

Papa and Uncle Ira led the way across the rock. Each time they came to a crack, Lily held onto Papa's hand to step over it. Joseph didn't want any help. He jumped back and forth over every crack as if they were the best part of the rock bed. Dannie tried to imitate Joseph but Papa held tightly to his hand while he jumped.

When they reached the middle of the rock bed, Mama spread out several blankets and Aunt Tillie unpacked the picnic basket. During the short, silent prayer before lunch, Lily thought she heard something—a funny noise, almost like a sad little cry. She strained her ears to hear it again. A pitiful little sound came from across the rock bed. This time Papa heard and snapped up his head. "What was that?" he asked.

"What was what?" Uncle Ira asked.

"I thought I heard something," Papa said. "It sounds like an animal is in some kind of distress."

"I heard it too," Lily said.

Everyone stopped to listen. There it was again! A sad, woebegone whimper. Papa walked around the rock bed and stopped at a big crack, peering down into it. "There's a little puppy down there!" he called back to them.

Joseph and Dannie dropped their chicken sandwiches and bolted over to Papa. Lily joined them. Joseph dropped to his knees to peer into the crack. "Let's rescue him!"

"We would need a ladder to get down to him," Papa said. "I didn't bring one along."

Joseph was horrified. "But we can't leave the puppy down there! It'll die."

"He does look hungry," Lily said. Joseph ran back to get the rest of his sandwich and tossed it down to the puppy. Lily was proud of Joseph's quick thinking. She knew how much he loved to eat. But she knew he loved animals even more than food.

Papa stroked his beard as he tried to think of what to do. "I'll drive down the road to the next farm and see if they have a ladder we can borrow."

"I'll go with you, Daniel," Uncle Ira said.

Joseph knelt at the edge of the crack and talked to the puppy in a soft, soothing voice. Lily took her sandwich and sat next to Joseph and Dannie by the crack. She felt sorry for the puppy as they waited for Papa to return. She wondered how long it had been trapped down there with no way to get out. Wasn't it amazing to think that today, of all days, was the day they had decided to drive to the rock bed? Just the day when a puppy needed to be rescued.

Papa and Uncle Ira came back with a ladder and lowered it carefully into the crack. Papa frowned. "I don't think this crack is wide enough for both me and the ladder."

"What if we turned it sideways?" Uncle Ira asked.

"There wouldn't be anything for it to lean against."

"I'll hold it upright," Uncle Ira said.

Papa looked doubtful. "You think you're strong enough?"

"I might be older than you are," Uncle Ira said. "But that doesn't mean I'm not just as strong as you are." To prove his point, Uncle Ira turned the ladder.

Papa flashed him a nervous look, then laughed, as he carefully stepped on the ladder and headed down into the crack. "Don't you let go, Brother Ira!"

Lily had the oddest feeling—Papa and Uncle Ira sounded just like Joseph and Dannie. She wondered if her brothers would still tease each other when they became grown men. Probably.

Everyone gathered around the crack to watch Papa climb down the ladder. Mama held her breath until Papa got to the bottom safely, then she let out a sigh of relief. Papa picked up the puppy and climbed back up. Before Papa reached the top step, Joseph reached out to get the puppy out of his arms. "Can I keep him?" he asked.

Over the top of Joseph's head, Papa and Mama exchanged a look. Lily never did understand what they said to each other in those looks; they had a language all their own. "We'll take him home with us today," Papa said. He stroked the puppy's head. "He certainly needs someone to take care of him. But we'll have to find out if he belongs to anyone else before we make any plans to keep him."

"We could put an ad in the newspaper to see if someone

has lost a puppy and wants it back," Mama said. She sounded as if she hoped the puppy might belong to someone else.

"If no one wants it, can we keep it?" Joseph asked. Lily knew what was coming. When it came to rescuing stray animals, Joseph wouldn't give up. He was worse than water wearing on a rock.

This sad puppy wasn't a puppy Lily would have picked for their family. It was scrawny and dirty, one ear drooped while the other one stood up in a point, and it had a black patch over one eye that gave it a cockeyed look, like a pirate.

"If no one claims it, then you get to keep it," Papa said.

Joseph hugged the puppy against his chest. "I'm going to call him Dozer."

"Wait," Lily said. "It's a boy puppy?"

Papa nodded. "Why Dozer?"

"Because it sounds strong," Joseph said. "Like a bulldozer."

Lily's heart sank. The last thing she needed was another strong-minded boy around the house.

4

Life with a Crazy Puppy

unt Tillie and Uncle Ira returned to Kentucky and life at Whispering Pines returned to normal. As normal as life could get with a crazy puppy at the farm.

One morning, Mama tied the apron filled with clothespins around Lily's waist. This apron was made just for laundry day. "I'll let you hang the rest of the things up by yourself," Mama said. "I'll go get the next load of laundry out of the washing machine."

The laundry basket was nearly empty; only a few towels, washcloths, and pairs of socks remained on the bottom. This, to Lily, was the best part of doing laundry. She didn't mind hanging things on the clothesline. She could be outside in the sunshine while she worked, and listen to the birds sing, and feel the gentle summer breeze.

Lily reached into the front of the apron, pulled out a clothespin, and bent down to get a towel out of the laundry basket. Dozer had been busy trying to catch his tail, and now he was lying on the grass watching Lily with his big puppy eyes.

When she lifted the towel, she shook it to flap out the wrinkles before she hung it on the line. Dozer sat up, interested. One of his ears twitched eagerly. He sprang to his feet as Lily lifted the towel to pin it to the clothesline. In the blink of an eye, he snatched the towel out of Lily's hands and bounded away with it.

"Hey!" Lily yelled. She chased after him. Dozer would stop, look at her as if to say, "You can't catch me!" and then dart off. The towel was dragged all over the muddy ground. It was filthy.

Lily stilled. Slowly, she inched her way toward Dozer and stepped on the edge of the towel. Then she reached down and tried to take it away from him. Dozer growled and wouldn't let it go. Lily was frustrated. This puppy was nothing but trouble and more trouble! And he was strong. Fast, too. Joseph had thought Dozer would be a good name because it sounded like a bold dog, but Lily could think of other names that would have fit him. Names like Rascal, Scamp, or Pest.

She walked back to the basement with one end of the towel in her hands. The other end was held by Dozer, still making deep growly sounds in his throat. Joseph tried to distract Dozer by throwing a ball. Dozer dropped the towel and bounded after the ball. Lily picked up the dirty, chewed towel with two fingers. It was disgusting. She took the towel into the basement to show Mama. "Dozer ran away with the towel," she said. "I think it needs to be washed again."

Mama sighed. "That little dog still needs a lot of training."

Lily agreed.

All week long, a heat wave had Cloverdale in its grip. By afternoon, it was too hot to be outside, so garden work needed to get done in the early morning. As soon as breakfast was over, Mama announced that they would be picking cucumbers this morning. "I want to can turmeric pickles," she told Lily, "so pick every cucumber that is over an inch long."

Turmeric pickles were some of Lily's favorites. She liked them much better than the salty-sour dill pickles that Papa liked so well. Picking cucumbers was always fun, easy work. She hurried to find several five-gallon pails to take out to the garden.

As Lily reached the garden, she set the pails down. Mama was peering over a cucumber vine, a puzzled look on her face. "How strange," she said. "I never saw anything like this."

Lily parted a cucumber vine to see what Mama was looking at. One bite was taken out of the cucumber. What kind of animal would do such a thing? Raccoons liked to eat sweet corn. Sometimes mice or moles liked to nibble on a few tomatoes and robins always liked strawberries, but she had never heard of any creature that took one bite out of cucumbers.

Mama and Lily spent the morning picking every single cucumber. They filled one pail with the unbitten ones. The bitten ones filled a second pail. "What a waste," Mama said sadly as she looked at all the ruined cucumbers.

It didn't take long to clean the pail of unbitten cucumbers and pack them into jars. It didn't take long because there weren't very many. Mama poured the turmeric spiced brine over the cucumbers and put them into the canner so the lids would seal. They were done by lunchtime, just as the heat of the day was in full force.

During lunch, Mama mentioned the mysterious half-eaten cucumbers. Joseph became very interested in the food on his plate.

A funny thought crossed Lily's mind. "Oh no! Was it Dozer?"

Joseph gave a slight half-shrug of his shoulder.

Papa saw. "Joseph, do you know anything about this?"

Joseph looked miserable. "I was hungry the other day, so I went to the garden and ate a cucumber. Dozer saw me eating it so he took a bite out of one, too. I thought it was funny but I didn't know he was going to take bites out of other cucumbers."

Papa finished chewing a slice of apple. "I've never known a dog to eat a cucumber."

Mama frowned. "That pup is more of a nuisance than any dog I have ever known."

Joseph's eyebrows shot up. He sent a pleading look to Papa. "He's only a puppy," Papa said, trying to reassure Mama. "We need to be patient while he learns how to become a good dog."

Mama didn't have much patience for mischievous animals, like goats or a bad puppy. Papa had all kinds of patience.

Lily thought she might be somewhere in between Papa and Mama. At times, Dozer could be fun, but she was getting tired of the trouble he caused. Especially when Mama pointed out that there wouldn't be many pickles to eat this winter.

The Magazine Article

apa brought the mail into the house and handed a letter to Mama. "What do you think, Rachel?"

Lily's ears perked up. Something interesting was in that letter. She watched carefully as Mama's eyes scanned the letter. She hoped her parents would discuss the letter now and not wait until they were alone.

Mama put the letter down. "Is it something you'd like to do?"

Do what? Lily wondered, but she knew she shouldn't ask. It wasn't her business.

"We don't have to make a decision right away," Papa said. "But it certainly is an offer to consider. It could help our business to have an article about our little woodworking shop in such a well-known magazine." He scanned the letter again. "I'm a little surprised Bill never mentioned he was a magazine writer when he was here with Ira and Tillie."

Now it made sense to Lily why that driver named Bill kept

commenting on Papa's business. He was thinking about writing an article about it.

The next day, Lily was happy to hear that Papa had decided to let Bill interview him about the woodworking shop. In the letter Papa wrote to Bill, he reminded him that the family would not pose for any pictures, but he was welcome to take pictures of the furniture Papa built and the workshop.

A few days later, Bill drove up in his green minivan. A big camera hung around his neck and a pad of paper was in his hand. The family was excited. That morning, Lily helped Mama bake cookies and make a special pudding of whipped Jell-O, cottage cheese, and fruit. The pleasant hum of machinery from Papa's woodworking shop in the basement filled the kitchen as they worked. Bill said it would take all day to gather information for his article so Mama invited him for lunch.

Lily placed the bowl of pudding in the refrigerator, floating it in a bigger bowl filled with ice water. Everything was ready for lunch, so Mama said she could watch Papa show Bill around the shop. Lily ran down the basement stairs, through the room filled with shelves of canned goods, and out to the shop. She didn't want to miss a moment of this special day.

Lily stood by the doorjamb and watched for a moment. She was surprised to see Bill take pictures of Papa as he cut out chair backs on the band saw. At one point, Papa noticed, too. He stopped his work and reminded Bill to not take pictures of him.

"Don't worry," Bill assured him. "I'm being very careful. All that I'm photographing is your hands while you're working."

Satisfied, Papa pulled the lever to start the band saw up again. Lily liked to watch as he guided the curved chair back. The band saw blade sliced easily through the wood. Somehow, Papa made his work seem as easy and effortless as play.

But the more Lily watched Bill, the more she was sure he was taking pictures of more than Papa's hands. She could tell his camera was aimed at Papa's face. Bill noticed Lily by the door and asked her to stand closer to Papa. Did he think she was dumb? She knew he wanted to take pictures of her, too.

Lily went upstairs to join Mama in the living room. She was sitting next to the window, sewing patches on Dannie's trousers in the afternoon sunlight. Dannie was hard on his trousers. His pants' knees were always needing new patches.

"Do you have something for me to sew?" Lily asked.

Mama tried to hide her surprise. Lily never, ever asked to help with sewing. Normally, she avoided sewing, but she'd rather be next to Mama, patching clothes, than be in the shop with Bill and his sneaky camera.

"There are several shirts that lost a button," Mama said, pointing to a pile of clothes on the chair next to her. "But I thought you wanted to spend the day in the shop with Papa."

Lily got the button basket from Mama's sewing machine desk and dug through the basket to find buttons that matched the shirt. Then the truth burst over her. "I don't trust Bill. He is taking pictures of Papa."

Mama's head snapped up in concern. "But Papa told him we don't want our pictures taken."

"I heard Papa tell him that just a little bit ago. Bill said he was only taking pictures of his hands," Lily said. "But I don't believe him."

"Lily, if Bill *said* he is only getting Papa's hands, you should believe him," Mama said gently. "We should believe the best in others."

Yes, it was nice to believe that, Lily thought, but not when your eyes told you to believe something else.

⁂

A few weeks later, when the mail arrived, Lily carried it to Mama. In it was Bill's magazine. Lily stood right next to Mama as she looked at the cover of the magazine. Mama opened the magazine, looked at the index, and gasped. There was a picture of Papa working in his shop and a short caption underneath it: *Discover the simple way craftsman Daniel Lapp builds beautiful furniture on page 43.*

Mama skimmed through the pages till she reached the article. Above the article was a big picture of the sign Papa had painted for their business. Behind the sign was a big white barn with red trim and a horse and buggy. Lily had never seen such a barn. It certainly wasn't the barn at Whispering Pines.

This hand-stenciled sign leads you to a hidden gem nestled in the mountains of Cloverdale, Pennsylvania, where an Amish family, Daniel and Rachel Lapp, have a woodworking shop in the basement of their rambling home.

They don't drive a car because their religion forbids the use of engines of any kind. When asked how he powered the machinery in his shop, Daniel took me outside where four draft horses were plodding in a circle, turning a handmade apparatus of gears and pulleys.

Daniel and his family have only recently moved to the Cloverdale area, but already he has built up a very successful business. "People like good, honest businesses," Daniel said, grinning ear-to-ear. "They like to know everything is made by hand." Like the chair seats. Each is made to fit perfectly as Daniel painstakingly whittles each seat to perfection with a draw knife.

Lies, lies! All lies. And Bill had, indeed, lied about taking pictures of Papa's hands. There were five pictures of Papa and one of Joseph and Dannie.

Mama tossed the magazine on the kitchen table. Her face looked drawn and tight. "Well, what do you think of that, Lily?"

"I wish Bill would never have come," Lily said. "He lied about everything."

Mama nodded. "He didn't get much right besides our names."

"Do you want me to go show it to Papa?"

"No," Mama said. "It's not worth interrupting his work. Let's put it aside for now and get supper ready. We'll talk about the article with Papa before bedtime."

As Lily peeled potatoes for supper, she felt sick to her stomach. She wasn't at all hungry. She wanted to run down to the shop and give Papa a big hug. He would feel awful about all the lies Bill had written about him.

Later that night, Papa sat in his chair with the magazine. He flipped through the pages until he came to the article and read it aloud so everyone could hear it.

The more Papa read, the more uneasy Lily felt—almost as if bugs were crawling all over her. Bill made the Lapp family sound silly and stupid. Imagine having draft horses walk in a circle to power a band saw! Ridiculous! She wondered how Papa could stay so calm as he read all of the lies.

"For more information about Daniel's furniture, write to: *Daniel Lapp, Cloverdale Route 2, Whispering Pines, PA.*"

Joseph snorted. "Even the address is wrong!"

Papa paged through the magazine. "Makes me wonder how much of this entire magazine is true," he said to no one in particular. He closed the magazine and looked at Lily and Joseph, gathered around his chair. "Bill wrote a lot of lies. We need to forgive him for what he did and pray for him. What I'd like to do is to toss this magazine in the woodstove and burn the article. I'd like to forget that Bill was ever here." He looked down at it for a long while, then stabbed it a few times with his finger. "But I think we'll keep it. It will be a good reminder to us whenever we're tempted to try to grow our business on our own instead of trusting God."

Saying Goodbye
to Grandpa Lapp

Sunlight flooded Lily's room and woke her. She jumped out of bed and crossed the room to open the window. She propped her elbows on the windowsill and rested her chin in her hands, gazing at Mama's flower bed next to the soft green grass of the yard. It was a beautiful Sunday morning in late August. Tomorrow, a new school term would start. She wondered what it would be like to have a new teacher.

Mama kept reassuring Lily that the new teacher was very nice, and that Lily would learn to love her just as much as she had loved Teacher Rhoda. Lily wasn't convinced. She still couldn't puzzle out why Teacher Rhoda wanted to up and marry Samuel Yoder, Aaron Yoder's oldest brother. Aaron was the worst boy in the entire world. The very thought of being permanently tied to any Yoder made her shudder. She had wanted to be like Teacher Rhoda in every way but that one. Never that.

Learning to love teachers hadn't worked very well for Lily. She had loved her first teacher, Ellen, and then along came Teacher Katie. She did not love Teacher Katie. She did not even like her. Now, she had grown to love her third teacher, Rhoda . . . but what if Teacher Judith was just like Teacher Katie? Maybe that was how it went: good, bad, good, bad. Teacher Judith lived in the neighboring church district and Lily had never met her. She hoped Teacher Judith didn't have big, bushy caterpillar eyebrows like Teacher Katie. For the second time that morning, Lily shuddered.

Her mind drifted to worrying about Effie Kauffman, the most annoying girl in all of Pennsylvania. Teacher Judith was going to board at Effie's house during the week. That was all Effie could talk about at church last Sunday—how she would help Teacher Judith check schoolbooks in the evenings and give her ideas about planning classes. Just the thought of Effie pawing through Lily's work made her hopping mad. She hoped Teacher Judith might have better sense than that.

Then her heart softened a little. How awful it would be to board at Effie Kauffman's home. Not only was there Effie to contend with, but her mother, Ida, too. She decided she would try to be especially helpful at school to make up for poor Teacher Judith's dreadful boarding situation. Maybe Mama would let Lily invite Teacher Judith to their house once a month for supper and an overnight. She would have to remember to ask Mama.

She watched a little brown sparrow fly onto the tip of a pine tree branch and sing a song. It was an off-Sunday, so Mama and Papa were still sleeping. She thought she might head downstairs soon and surprise Mama by starting breakfast. Just as she put her hand on her doorknob, she heard the sound of a car turning into the driveway. She ran back to the window and recognized the big blue station wagon of Mr. Tanner, a hired driver. Lily wondered why he would come to their home so early on a Sunday morning. An odd feeling ran through her—a feeling of dread—and she didn't know why. Lily ran down the stairs and knocked on Mama and Papa's bedroom door. "Mr. Tanner is here," she called. She could hear Papa's feet hit the floor, then his footsteps as he hurried to the door.

Papa rushed outside to see what Mr. Tanner wanted. Lily followed behind. Mr. Tanner opened his car door and stepped out when he saw them coming toward him. "Good morning, Daniel," he said. "I came to bring you a message."

Mr. Tanner's voice, usually so jolly, sounded serious and sad. "Your brother Ira called me this morning." He paused and looked down at his shoes. "He said your daddy passed away last night."

Grandpa Lapp was dead? It couldn't be true! He couldn't die. Lily had never even finished the scrapbook she had started as a surprise for Grandpa and Grandma. Now he would never see it.

Mr. Tanner said he was sorry to bring sad news. He and Papa spoke for a few more minutes, then he got back in his car and drove away. Papa and Lily walked back into the house, silent and solemn. Papa drew out a chair from the kitchen table and sat down, holding his forehead in his hands. Big tears started to run down his cheeks. Lily had never seen Papa cry before, not once. Big choking sobs rose from Lily's belly and Papa held his arms out to her. She scrambled into his lap and cried right alongside him.

A few minutes later, Joseph and Dannie galloped down the stairs and into the kitchen, like it was just another summer day. But it wasn't. Mama followed behind the boys, telling them to be quiet because baby Paul was sleeping. They all ground to a halt when they saw Papa and Lily crying at the table.

Papa looked at Mama. "My father died." The boys burst into tears and scrambled to find a spot on Papa's lap—pushing Lily off, but she didn't mind. They all loved Grandpa Lapp. Papa took his handkerchief out of his pocket and wiped his tears. He patted Lily's cheeks with the handkerchief and then the boys' cheeks.

Papa gently shooed Joseph and Dannie off his lap. "I need to go milk Pansy." He stood and put an arm around Mama. "We need to get ready to go to Kentucky. Mr. Tanner offered to take us to the funeral. He'll be here around one o'clock to pick us up."

Mama wiped tears from her eyes and nodded. As Papa went out to the barn, she watched him through the window. Lily wondered what she was thinking. Finally, Mama turned to Lily. "Go up to the attic, Lily, and bring down the big black suitcase while I start to prepare breakfast."

Breakfast? Who could eat? Lily was sure no one would want to eat anything. Grandpa Lapp was dead! But she went upstairs to get the suitcase for Mama.

❧

In just a few hours, Mama had everything planned. Uncle Jacob would take care of the animals while the family traveled to Kentucky to attend Grandpa Lapp's funeral. Baby Paul would stay at Grandma and Grandpa Miller's. Lily knew Aunt Susie would have fun helping Grandma take care of him.

Mama had everything packed and ready by one o'clock, when Mr. Tanner drove up to the house. Papa and Dannie sat up front with Mr. Tanner while Mama, Lily, and Joseph sat in the back. The long ride was very quiet.

It was after midnight by the time the family arrived at Grandma Lapp's house. It felt awful to Lily to be here and know that Grandpa Lapp wasn't here anymore. She wondered if Papa had the same thought.

A dim light shone from a kitchen window and the front door opened as Mr. Tanner's car pulled into the driveway. Uncle Ira came out to greet them, carrying a big flashlight.

Uncle Ira spoke to Papa in low, hushed tones, like a whisper. "So glad you could come here so quickly," he said. "Dad's passing was quite a shock to all of us. There'd been no warning that he had any heart trouble until he had the heart attack last night."

Uncle Ira led the way into the house and showed Papa and Mama where they could sleep. "I'll make some nests on the floor in the storage room for the children to sleep," he said. He opened the door to the storage room and lifted the lid to a cedar chest that was tucked under a window. He pulled several blankets out and plopped them on the floor. "There you go. See you in the morning." He clumped away down the stairs.

Lily looked at her blanket nest. She was used to making a nest on the floor, but this was not much of a nest. It was just a heavy comforter. There was no pillow or a quilt to cover her. Joseph and Dannie were so tired that they just lay down and curled up like two puppies. Mama turned to the cedar chest again to try to find quilts and pillows. She pulled out two blankets and gave one to Lily and one to Joseph and Dannie to share.

Mama hunted around the room. "I can't seem to find any pillows, so we'll just have to make our own." She showed Lily how to roll up one end of a comforter to make a pillow.

Lily lay down. The makeshift pillow felt lumpy and uncomfortable. Everything smelled of cedar and mothballs. It made her feel sick and she was sure she would never sleep. Joseph and Dannie were snoring like the little piglets at Hannah's farm. She rolled over once, then twice, and then it was morning.

Lily's eyes burst open at the sound of a rooster crowing his good morning to the world. For one moment, she was home at Whispering Pines, waiting to hear the familiar sounds that meant Mama was in the kitchen. Then the rooster crowed again, and she knew she wasn't home. This rooster's crow was the sound of a bantam rooster, which was smaller than a chicken and louder than two. She took a deep breath and smelled mothballs. It all came to her—she was in Kentucky at Grandma Lapp's house, sleeping on the floor in a room filled with mothballs. She couldn't wait to get up and go outside and breathe fresh air.

When the bantam rooster crowed again, Joseph and Dannie woke up. The three of them dressed and went down to the kitchen. Grandma Lapp was waiting for them, sitting in Grandpa's creaky old rocking chair, slowly rocking back and forth. She spread her arms wide open and they rushed to her.

Breakfast was scarcely over when women from Grandma's church started to arrive. They scurried around to start washing windows. Lily knew what this meant. All day, the women would be cleaning the house. The walls and ceilings would be washed, the floors would be waxed, every horizontal surface would be dusted. The women in the church would help to prepare the house and cook the meal for Grandpa Lapp's funeral. It was what women did.

Since Lily and Mama were relatives, they weren't expected to help clean. Instead, Papa and Mama sat next to Grandma and quietly visited. Lily, Joseph, and Dannie sat on a bench against the wall, quiet as mice, bored as could be. Some women and teenaged girls started to wash the walls of the living room. Lily wished she could help them. Anything would be better than just sitting. Just sitting and sitting. Boring!

It wasn't long before Joseph and Dannie couldn't stand it any longer. Joseph placed one hand on the bench between them, and Dannie placed his hand on top of it. Joseph placed his hand on top of Dannie's, and Dannie placed his other hand on top of it. It was the stacking game. Joseph pulled his hand from the bottom of the stack and placed it on top. Then Dannie did the same. Then Joseph did. Then Dannie did. Faster and faster until their hands were just a blur. Papa frowned at the noise they were making. They stopped. Lily, Joseph, and Dannie sat quietly with their hands in their laps. Bored stiff.

⋇

By late afternoon, vans started to arrive. One after the other, filled with Papa's brothers and sisters and their children. Men had brought church benches to the house and filled the living room with them. The benches at the back of the room started to fill with Lily's cousins, aunts, and uncles.

Lily didn't know any of her same-age cousins except for three: Ella, Rosie, and Miriam. She knew those cousins only because they were included in her circle letter. She wished the girl cousins could go find a place to talk far away from this room of hushed whispers. Everyone acted sad and solemn and oh-so-proper.

Happily, all the cousins—boys and girls—were just as bored as Lily. The boys lasted about an hour and then they suddenly got up and filed out to the barn. Papa gave a nod to Joseph and Dannie and they followed right behind the big boys.

The girl cousins, being more mature and grown-up than the boys, sat for a while longer, until one of the older ones suggested that they could go outside and sit under a shade tree. Everyone else jumped up from the hard backless benches, as if they were set free. Lily was so relieved when Mama said she could go, too. Oh, to be able to get up and walk outside! She had never appreciated it so much.

The boy cousins had gathered outside the barn, talking and laughing. The girls sat under the big shade trees, clumped together in little age groups.

Lily sat on the ground next to Rosie, her closest-in-age cousin. "I wish we didn't have to miss our first day of school," Rosie said.

Lily's eyes went wide. Today was the first day of school! How could she have forgotten such an important day? Her thoughts left Kentucky and sailed to Cloverdale. How were Hannah and Beth and Malinda doing with a new teacher? Where was Lily's seat? It had better not be anywhere near Aaron Yoder. She was so sad to realize she had missed out on the excitement of the first day of school. Effie, she knew, would be acting insufferably important. She would want everyone to assume she was Teacher Judith's best friend.

"How many children are in your grade?" Miriam asked her.

Surely, Miriam was interested only in the girls in Lily's grade. Who would ever care about the stupid boys? Hannah did, but she had an unreasonable crush on Aaron Yoder. Effie would care about the stupid boys, but she was boy crazy and made no sense at all. "There are four other girls in my grade," Lily said. Rosie and Ella had about the same number of girls in their grades.

Miriam sighed wistfully. "I wish I had classmates," she said. "I'm all alone in my grade. There are plenty of children in the grade ahead and behind me. I'd even be happy with a boy in my class."

Lily knew Miriam wouldn't feel that way if she could spend a day anywhere near Aaron Yoder or Sam Stoltzfus. She was just about to say so when something started pinging around them. Someone was tossing gravel peas at the girls' heads. The girls sprang to their feet and looked up into the leafy tree branches. Rosie's brother, Ben, was high on a branch, laughing as he reached into his pants pocket to toss another handful of gravel at them.

"Oh Ben!" Rosie said. "Go away and quit being such a big pest."

Ben took his time climbing back down the tree. When he hit the ground, he hooked his thumbs into his suspenders. "Do you girls want to play hide and seek?"

"We'll play if the older girls will," Rosie said.

Lily thought that was pretty smart of Rosie. If they ended up in trouble for playing during the preparation for Grandpa Lapp's funeral, the older girls would be held responsible.

"No problem," Ben said. "I'll go find everyone."

For the first time since yesterday morning, Lily felt happy. She liked being a part of a big group of cousins. By the time Ben rounded up everyone who wanted to play hide-and-seek, he had gathered twenty-two children. All of Lily's first cousins on the Lapp side who were close to her in age. Since it had been Ben's idea to play hide-and-seek, the oldest cousins said he should be the one to do the seeking. Ben was pleased. Lily could tell that he liked being the center of attention. He reminded her of the horrible Aaron Yoder.

"I'm only going to count to one hundred before I start looking for all of you," Ben said. He buried his face in the crook of his arm and leaned against the tree trunk. "One . . . two . . . three . . ."

Ella spoke first. "Let's all hide in the woodshed." Miriam, Rosie, Lily, and Ella held hands and ran across the yard toward the woodshed. As they reached the shed, Rosie lifted the hook that held the door shut. The girls stepped inside and drew the door shut behind them. As Lily's eyes adjusted to the dim light, she felt an unexpected wave of missing her grandfather. Grandpa Lapp had hung his gardening tools in a row on one wall. Along another wall were neatly stacked piles of split firewood that reached all the way to the roof. Papa stacked his wood in the exact same way. Another wave of missing Grandpa crashed over her. Then it vanished, like a wisp of steam from a cup of tea, as they heard Ben's voice call out, looking for people. The girls froze, huddling low on the floor so Ben couldn't see them through the tiny window as he ran by.

A few seconds later, Lily heard a funny little noise outside the shed. The girls looked at each other. "Was that the hook on the door?" Lily asked. Ben's face appeared at the tiny window as he peered inside and then ran away, laughing as he went.

Rosie tried to open the door but it was locked. "Ben!" she hollered. "Get back here and let us out!" She started to pound on the door. "Grrrr! He is such a pest!"

Why, this was just the kind of thing Aaron Yoder liked to do! Lily hoped that Ben and Aaron Yoder never met. Double trouble.

The girls took turns pounding on the door. Finally, the door hook was undone. Mama opened the door with a look of frustration. She spoke directly to Lily. "I don't mind if you want to play with your cousins instead of sitting inside, but I expect you to be quiet. Understand?"

"Yes, Mama," Lily said. How unfair! Why was she the only one who was told to be quiet? Her cousins made just as much noise as she had. Rosie and Ben were the loudest of all.

❦

The next morning, after breakfast, Mama helped Lily pin her black cape and apron. All the other Lapp aunts and girl cousins were arriving soon. Buggies drove up to the house to drop off women and girls. Everyone was dressed in black and no one smiled. Even though it was a warm day, Lily felt cold.

Aunt Tillie, as usual, told everyone what to do and where to sit. All the older grandchildren were supposed to sit on benches at the back of the room. Lily was happy to see she could sit on a bench against the wall. She looked forward to leaning against the wall during the long service. The girls filed in first and then the boys.

Cousin Ben sat right in front of Lily. He looked as if he had

58

been doing somersaults in the hayloft before he had come into the house. His hair had a few pieces of hay sticking out of it.

After everyone had been seated, the bishop stood and started to preach. Little by little, Ben leaned on his bench so his backside was resting against Lily's knees. Lily wasn't sure what to do. Rosie noticed and nudged Ben. He looked back at both girls with a smug "you can't tell me what to do" grin on his freckled face. He sat up, but it wasn't long before he started pushing his backside against Lily's knees again. Disgusted, Rosie nudged him to sit forward again. It worked . . . for another minute. Then he leaned again.

Rosie leaned over to whisper in Lily's ear. "Poke him with a pin the next time he leans against your knees."

What a good idea! Lily wished she could think quickly like that. She pulled a pin from her apron belt and held it by her knees. It wasn't long before Ben tried to lean back again. This time, Lily was ready. She held the pin firmly in her hands, point side out, and felt a delightful thrill of triumph as Ben jumped to his feet when the pin stuck him.

Ben's commotion caused his parents to swivel around. His father rose to his feet and marched to the back of the room. He placed his hand on the back of Ben's neck and guided him to sit between his parents.

The pin had worked! Lily tried not to feel smug as the back of Ben's neck flushed bright red with embarrassment.

❧

Lily sat in the buggy with Papa and Mama and the boys as they made their way to the graveyard, slowly and sadly. Ahead of them was the buggy with the casket that held Grandpa Lapp's body. Next came the buggies with Papa's older brothers and sisters. Behind them came Papa's two younger sisters, then a long string of buggies filled with other relatives and friends.

At the edge of Grandpa Lapp's grave, Lily stood next to Papa and watched as four men gently lowered the casket and covered it with dirt. The sound of the dirt hitting the casket made Lily cringe. It took a long time until the men were done. Finally, everyone returned to the house to eat a meal that the women had prepared.

It was always strange to Lily that grown-ups returned from a burial acting happy. Just a short time ago, everyone had been sad and crying. Now, they were laughing and talking and eating.

Lily sat at a table with her girl cousins, eating and laughing. She was looking forward to an afternoon filled with fun as soon as they could all go outside to play.

Suddenly, Papa was at her side. "It's time to start for home."

So soon? Lily had just felt as if she was finally getting to know her cousins. She rose from the table and hugged her cousins goodbye.

On the ride home in Mr. Tanner's big blue station wagon, Lily had so many feelings stirring inside of her. She was sad that she would never see Grandpa Lapp again. It was hard to say goodbye to Grandma Lapp. But she did enjoy visiting with her Lapp cousins. She couldn't wait for the next circle letter—it would be so much more fun now that she was familiar with her cousins. And then there was school to look forward to. She was eager to meet Teacher Judith. She was even curious about how puffed up Effie would act at school.

It was tiring, in a way, to have so many thoughts bouncing around Lily's head. Soon, she closed her eyes and fell asleep.

Lily's First Day of School

Lily's toes couldn't stop tapping under the breakfast table. She was eager to get to school today. She had missed two full days and she was full of worry. Would she be far behind her class? What if Teacher Judith thought she should stay in fourth grade for a little while longer?

And then she started to worry about Teacher Judith. What kind of a teacher would she be? What if she didn't excuse Lily for her grandfather's funeral? What if she was mad at Lily for being gone? And stayed mad all year?

Then there were other worries. Where would Lily's desk be? If it were anywhere near Aaron Yoder's, she thought she might scream, right then and there.

But if she did, then Teacher Judith would think she was crazy.

Oh, there was so much to worry about when you were in fifth grade.

She couldn't stand it any longer. "Mama, can Joseph and I go to school early?"

Joseph's spoon froze, midair. "Why?" He stuffed the spoonful of porridge in his mouth.

"Why? Why! Because it's the first day!" Lily couldn't understand why Joseph didn't like school. She loved school. There were some parts of school she didn't love, like the Aaron Yoder and Effie Kauffman parts, but other than that, she loved everything about it. Joseph was the opposite. He disliked everything about school except for recess.

"As soon as Joseph is done with his breakfast," Mama said, "you can both go."

Lily stared at Joseph until he shoveled down the last bite. After a silent prayer bookended the meal—the family prayed before and after, giving thanks and returning thanks—Lily grabbed her bonnet and lunch box and hurried down the driveway. If she ran, she would arrive at school all damp and sweaty, but she did walk briskly. Joseph dragged behind like he was heading to church.

She hoped she might be the first in the schoolhouse, but Effie Kauffman was already there, sweeping the room. Effie gave Lily a sweet-as-pie smile when she saw her. "Well, look here, Teacher Judith," she said, very prim. "Lily Lapp has finally decided to come to school."

Typical Effie.

Teacher Judith was at her desk. She looked up and gave Lily a smile. "Welcome, Lily. Don't you have a brother?"

"Joseph. He's out on the playground."

"Effie, show Lily where her desk is so she can put her things away."

Effie dropped the broom and sailed across the room to a

desk against the wall. "This is where you sit, Lily." She opened the lid for Lily. As Lily put her pencils and crayon box into the desk, Effie whispered, "Don't you wonder where Aaron is sitting?"

"No," Lily said. As long as he wasn't next to her.

"Hannah sits right next to you, then Beth, then Malinda, then me. Right behind me is . . . Aaron!" Effie was delighted to be near Aaron, all year long.

Lily was just as delighted to be far, far away from Aaron. She was on the other side of the room. How wonderful! Fifth grade was looking promising.

"Teacher Judith is giving a big prize to the student with perfect attendance," Effie said. "But you—" she pointed to Lily—"have already lost it."

Lily was so disappointed! She would have loved to win a

prize for perfect attendance. She had never won a prize at school, as hard as she tried.

Effie traced a finger around the back of Lily's seat. "I suppose you heard that Hannah's farm sold and that she's moving in a few weeks."

Lily's eyes went wide. She had pushed the whole thought of Hannah's move out of her mind. Effie could see this was news to Lily. "Oh, I thought you knew! I thought Hannah told you everything." She gave Lily a fake smile. Then she spotted Aaron and Sam on the playground and flounced outside. Aaron saw Lily through the window and made monkey ears at her.

Lily's happiness over the first day of school popped like a balloon. Effie and Aaron had that effect on her, many times. She finished organizing her things in her desk and went outside to wait for her friends to arrive.

Beth and Malinda were coming up the road and ran to greet Lily when they saw her sitting on the schoolhouse steps. "Welcome home!" Beth said.

Malinda peered anxiously into Lily's face. "Was the funeral for your grandfather very, very sad?"

"It was a little sad," Lily said. "But it was fun to visit with my cousins." The three girls sat on the steps, warmed by the morning sunshine. "Teacher Judith seems nice." She was older than Lily thought she would be, and much bigger than she had expected. Low in the backside and high in the front side and rather bunched up in the middle.

"She is nice," Beth said. She looked behind her to make sure the schoolhouse door was closed. "She doesn't have any rules."

"None?" Lily said.

"Not a one," Malinda said. "She said she's sure we'll all behave because we *want* to, not because we *have* to."

Lily squinted her eyes in disbelief. "Didn't anyone warn her about Aaron Yoder and Sam Stoltzfus?"

Beth snorted. "She's living with Effie Kauffman. Teacher Judith probably heard the sun rose and set by Aaron."

Hannah and Levi came around the bend. Hannah broke into a run to join the girls on the steps. "Lily! I'm glad you're back! I have news."

"I already heard," Lily said glumly.

Beth, Malinda, and Hannah exchanged a look. "Effie," all three girls said, at the same time. Effie Kauffman liked to be the first to know everything, often before it happened.

"When do you move?" Lily asked.

Hannah sat down beside her. "In a few weeks."

Lily wished Hannah didn't look so excited. The thought of Hannah moving away made Lily want to cry.

Just then, Effie came toward the girls from the playground, waddling like she was very fat. Hannah frowned. "She's imitating Teacher Judith. She's been doing that since school started."

"I thought she liked Teacher Judith," Lily said. "I thought she would like having her stay at her house."

Hannah shrugged. "She does. She just makes fun of her behind her back."

"That's Effie," Beth said. Malinda nodded.

Two-faced Effie.

※◦◦⚬◦

The next morning, as Lily and Joseph walked to school, they chatted about the writing assignment Teacher Judith had given to them. Each student was supposed to write a short story about something that had happened to them during the summer. The student who had written the best story would receive a prize.

Lily liked to write. She liked prizes even better, though she had never won anything. But trying to think of something interesting that had happened was harder than she had thought it would be.

She practically tripped and realized her shoelace had come untied. She set her lunch box down and bent down to tie it while Joseph waited for her. Lily finished tying her lace and straightened up just in time to see a dog charging toward her. Not just any dog. A Dozer dog.

Dozer jumped all over them, wagging his tail and wiggling all over. "Go home, Dozer," Joseph said sternly, pointing toward home. Dozer didn't understand. He tried to grab Joseph's hand with his mouth as if he thought there was a treat in it.

"Go back, Dozer!" Lily shouted. She and Joseph stamped their feet and pretended to chase him. Dozer would run a few feet and start following them again.

"Dozer is a dumb dog," Lily said.

"No he isn't," Joseph said, offended. "He's very smart. He wants to be with me."

Lily knew it was pointless to argue about Dozer with Joseph. He was crazy about that puppy.

They heard the school bell ring and ran the rest of the way to school. Lily was glad the other children were already in the schoolhouse. No one had seen Dozer follow them to school. Nobody's dog ever did that. Surely, Dozer would get tired of waiting outside the schoolhouse for Joseph and go back home again.

But when the first recess came, Dozer was waiting patiently under the tree in the school yard. When he saw Joseph, he ran over to greet him. Just as Lily feared, Aaron Yoder noticed. "That's the strangest looking dog I've ever seen," Aaron said. "His ears are funny and he has a black patch over his eye like a pirate." He nudged Sam Stoltzfus and the two started pointing and laughing at Dozer. "What a weird-looking dog!"

Now wait just a minute. Lily thought Dozer was dumb and she thought he was a little strange looking, but she wasn't going to let anybody—especially Aaron Yoder—call *her* dog names. She marched up to Aaron and Sam.

"Stop making fun of our dog."

Aaron couldn't wipe the grin off his sassy face. "What's that weird-looking dog's name?"

"His name is Dozer," Joseph said, stroking the top of Dozer's head.

Aaron doubled over and laughed some more. "Dozer . . . His name is Dozer! What a dumb name for a dog."

"A dumb name for a dumb dog," Sam echoed.

It took a lot to get Joseph riled. He was like Papa that way. But Aaron Yoder had done it. Joseph's hands were clenched in fists by his sides. "Dozer is not a dumb name, and he is not a dumb dog. He's my dog."

Aaron Yoder just kept laughing, like a hyena, and suddenly Joseph punched him right in the nose. Aaron stopped laughing. Sam stilled, and all motion on the school ground stopped. Everything was silent. Even the birds had stopped singing in the trees. Wide-eyed, Joseph stood there shaking his hurting hand, awaiting his fate. Even Dozer sensed something was going on and snuggled tightly against Joseph's legs.

The unnatural silence beckoned Teacher Judith from her

desk. She popped her head out the window and said, "What's going on out here?"

Effie, the bearer of all news, true or otherwise, said, "Joseph punched Aaron right in the nose."

Teacher Judith hurried outside. She peered at Aaron's nose, trying to see if it was broken or swelling up. She didn't know what to do next. Lily figured she probably hadn't had to deal with nose punching before. "It's okay," Aaron said, waving her away. "I was teasing him about his dog." He glanced at Joseph, still holding onto his nose. "Sorry about that."

Aaron Yoder never apologized for any crime he committed, not unless a teacher made him. The world was turning upside down and Lily didn't know what to make of it.

Teacher Judith gathered her wits about her. "Joseph, I want you to apologize to Aaron for hitting him."

Joseph scuffed the gravel with the toe of his shoe. "I'm sorry I hit you," he said, though he didn't sound too terribly sorry to Lily. He walked off to join his friends and Dozer trotted behind, jumping and oblivious to the chaos he'd created.

❧

Papa had an idea to keep Dozer from following Lily and Joseph to school. Each morning, he kept Dozer in the woodworking shop until Lily and Joseph were safely in school.

Papa's plan worked for a few days. Lily thought Dozer might be teachable after all, until the day when Dozer sneaked into the schoolhouse during lunch. Everyone was quietly eating when Sam Stoltzfus suddenly let out a yelp. "Hey! Get that dog away from me!"

Lily looked over at Sam's desk, and there was Dozer, calmly finishing off the last of Sam's sandwich. If it hadn't been

Dozer, she might have had a good laugh over the sight of Sam, looking so indignant, as Dozer polished off his sandwich. But since it was Dozer, she couldn't enjoy the moment.

≈≈≈

It was a sunny Tuesday in September. Mama checked each pin in Lily's dress to make sure they fit neatly. "Okay, Lily, I think you're ready to go." Lily wished Mama meant she could go to school, but there would be no school today. The whole community was taking a day off school and work to help Uncle Elmer and his family load a semi with their belongings. They had sold their farm and were moving to live with Hannah's grandparents on her father's side. Uncle Elmer would manage his parents' farm.

Lily ran out the door to join Papa and Joseph and Dannie. Mama decided to stay home with little Paul. "I don't want to see them leave," Mama had admitted at breakfast. "We said our goodbyes last evening when they were all here for supper, and I don't think I can say goodbye again." It looked as if Mama was trying not to cry. She was going to miss her sister Mary as much as Lily would miss her cousin Hannah.

But Lily felt differently about saying goodbye. She was sad, so sad, that Hannah was moving, but she wanted to spend every minute with her before she left. It would be a long time before she could see her again.

When Papa steered Jim into the driveway, Lily was dismayed to see horses and buggies parked everywhere, filling Uncle Elmer's driveway. As soon as Papa said she could go, Lily jumped off the buggy, ducked around people, and ran into the house to find Hannah. The house was strange, empty, and echoey. Boxes were piled along the wall beside the front door, waiting to be carried out. Men carried furniture out to the waiting semitrailer.

Aunt Mary spotted Lily from across the kitchen. "Hannah is upstairs in her room."

Lily flew up the stairs. Her heart caught when she saw Hannah's room. Her bed and dresser were gone. She was removing her clothes from the closet and folding them neatly before she placed them in a box. Lily quietly sat down beside her and helped fold clothes. It didn't take long until that job was done, but they didn't know what to do next. They went downstairs, but there were so many people milling around the house that they kept getting in the way, so finally they went back to Hannah's room and sat on the floor to talk. The only problem was that they had nothing to say to each other. Too sad.

By noon, the trailer was filled. Everyone gathered to eat sandwiches and cookies that the women had brought along. Too soon, lunch was over. Now it was really time to say goodbye.

The women murmured comforting words to Aunt Mary. "God bless you in your new home. I hope you'll be very happy as you adjust to a new community. Safe travels. Come back to visit often." Aunt Mary shook each person's hand, thanking them for helping, saying goodbye.

Lily gave Hannah a hug. Tears started to sting her eyes and she tried to blink faster to hide them. A little part of her felt bothered that Hannah didn't seem nearly as sad about leaving as Lily was to see her go.

As Hannah and her family walked out the door to leave, Lily understood why Mama didn't want to have to watch them go. She couldn't stand it, either. While the rest of the community waved goodbye as the van and trailer drove away, Lily ran up the stairs into Hannah's empty room. She opened the closet door and sat on the floor. The tears that had threatened to come all morning were here now, and she couldn't stop them.

After Lily had cried herself out, she wiped her face with her apron. She knew that the women had planned to wash all the walls, windows, and floors after Uncle Elmer's family left. They wanted to get the house ready for the new family that was moving in tomorrow. How awful it would be if the women opened up Hannah's closet and found Lily sobbing.

Slowly, she peeped her head out the closet door. To her horror, David Yoder, Aaron's father, stood in the middle of the room. He looked surprised to see Lily's head emerge out of the closet. "I just wanted to walk through the house to make sure they didn't forget anything before the new family moves in," he said. He glanced around the room. "It looks like they forgot to take a thermometer." He plucked a heart-shaped thermometer off the wall and handed it to Lily. "You can take this home with you and hang it on your wall. That way, every time you see it, you can feel good about taking care of something for Hannah until you see her again. You can give it to her the next time you see her. Maybe it will help you to not miss her quite as much."

Lily took the thermometer from David Yoder and hugged it close to her. She was sure he must be one of the kindest men she had ever met. As kind as Papa. He could understand how sad she was feeling and tried to make her feel better without embarrassing her. Just the opposite of his son. How disappointed he must be to have a son like Aaron.

Lily knew she should probably help the women and girls

clean the house, but she couldn't stay any longer. She found her bonnet from the closet shelf and went to find Papa to tell him that she was going home. That was fine with him. Papa understood, just like David Yoder. Hannah was like a sister to Lily.

Mama was surprised to see Lily when she got home. She smiled when Lily showed Hannah's thermometer to her and told her what David Yoder had said. "That sounds like a good idea," Mama said. "I'll help you hang it on your bedroom wall right away. I think Hannah would be pleased."

Mama helped Lily select the best spot in her room and pounded a nail into the bedroom wall. Lily hung the thermometer carefully on it. Mama and Lily sat on the bed and looked at it. Somewhere out there, Hannah and the rest of her family were in a van traveling far away to their new home, but a part of her remained behind in that little heart-shaped thermometer. It made Lily feel better just looking at it. She wondered if it helped Mama, too.

The sweet moment was broken when Paul picked up the hammer and started to pound the floor, making dents.

Mama jumped off the bed and took the hammer from Paul. "I think it's time to get to work. I want to bake an extra batch of gingersnap cookies to take along tomorrow when we help the new family move in. Who knows, Lily? Maybe you'll end up with a special new friend."

Harvey Hershberger
Moves to Town

Lily sat in her desk at school and tried to concentrate on studying her German spelling, but she couldn't stop glancing over at the empty desk next to her. Hannah's desk. She wondered if Hannah had started school today.

Then her thoughts drifted over to the new family that was moving into Hannah's house today. She wondered if the family had already unloaded their belongings. Papa and Mama were going to spend the day helping them.

Lily thought there shouldn't be school today. She thought it would be nice if everyone could be there to help them move in and welcome them to Cloverdale, but Papa said that the only time school was canceled was when someone got married, someone died, or someone moved away. Everyone needed to say goodbye. But when a person moved in, there would be plenty of people there to help unload the truck without the school children underfoot. There would be plenty more time to say hello and get acquainted later on.

Lily wondered how many children might be in the new family and if one of them might sit in Hannah's empty desk. In a way, she hoped so. In another way, she hoped not.

꽃

The next morning, as Lily finished drying the last breakfast dish, she looked out the window to see if she could catch any sight of those new children as they walked to school. Were they feeling nervous about starting a new school?

Lily would never forget how she had felt when she first moved to Cloverdale and had to walk into a classroom filled with strangers staring curiously at her. Her head felt light and her hands were icy cold and she thought she might throw up, right in front of everyone. She hoped the new children weren't feeling as anxious as she had been. Mama had told her there were many children in the family, including girls, but she couldn't remember if one was Lily's age. It was disappointing to Lily that Mama wouldn't have made a point to find out that particular piece of information. Lily couldn't wait to meet these new girls. The new girls would never take Hannah's place, but it was always, always a good thing to have more girls in school.

Lily peered out the window to see if the new children had started up the road yet. Mama had told them to stop at Whispering Pines so Joseph and Lily could show them the way to school. So far, there was no sign of them. She hoped they wouldn't be late. "Mama, what are the girls' names?"

"I don't remember," Mama said. "There were so many children I couldn't keep track of everyone's names or ages. I do remember the names of the parents: Abe and Clara Hershberger."

"I like that last name," Dannie said. "It sounds like a chocolate burger. Hershey burger." He hopped around the kitchen on one leg, chanting "Hershey burger, Hershey burger, chocolate, chocolate Hershey burgers."

Lily frowned at Dannie. He listened in to every conversation she and Mama had. She wondered how Mama could be so patient with him, all day long.

Mama only laughed at Dannie. "Chocolate burgers sound rather unappetizing to me, especially after breakfast."

When Dannie kept chanting "Hershey burger," Lily finally put a stop to it. She had caught sight of the children walking up the road and didn't want them to hear Dannie bungling their name. Once he got something into his head, it was hard to change it. "Dannie, their last name is 'Hershberger.' Not 'Hershey burger.'"

Lily grabbed her bonnet and lunch box and tossed a hurried goodbye to Mama and Dannie. She ran down to the basement to tell Joseph it was time to meet the new children and show them the way to school.

As usual, Joseph was in no hurry to get to school. Slowly, he plucked his hat off the wall peg by the door. "Hurry, Joseph," Lily said. She couldn't wait to meet these girls!

Lily and Joseph ran to the end of the driveway and stopped abruptly. There were six children standing at the edge of Whispering Pines' driveway: an older girl, a passel of boys, and two little girls.

For once, Lily was glad that Joseph wasn't shy. He walked right up to them. "Hi," he said. "I'm Joseph and this is Lily. Who are you?"

The tallest girl spoke first. "I'm Becky. I'm in eighth grade."
She pointed to a boy. "That's Harvey. He's in sixth grade.
Junior is in fourth grade. Andy is in second. And Carrie and
Mary are twins. They're in first grade."

Becky's eyes left Lily and Joseph and darted down the road,
where Aaron, Sam, and Sam's brother, Ephraim, had emerged
from a shortcut in the woods to reach the road. Lily tried
hard to cover her disappointment. Becky was not interested
in her at all, and there were no other girls near Lily's age.

As Lily said hello to each child, she was shocked when
Harvey winked at her. No one else seemed to notice, but she
thought he was very bold. She quickly looked away but not
before she felt her cheeks grow warm.

On the way to the schoolhouse, Becky asked Lily about
the other eighth graders. "I'm sorry to say there are only two
boys," Lily said, and thought it was odd that Becky seemed
pleased with that news. "Ephraim Stoltzfus and Wall-Eyed
Walter."

"Wall-Eyed Walter?" Becky repeated.

"We're not supposed to call him that, but everybody does,"
Joseph piped up. "Walter's got a wandering eye. He's a little
. . . different."

Becky squinted. "How so?"

"His mind circles a little slow," Joseph said, "but it eventu-
ally gets there."

For the rest of the walk, Harvey did all the talking. Becky
looked bored. Teacher Judith was on the school steps, waiting to show the new children to their desks. As each child
settled into the desks, the schoolhouse was bursting at the
seams. All empty seats were now full. Lily glanced all around
the room, liking the extra noise and activity. Then her eyes

met Harvey's and he gave her a foxy grin with a wink. Lily snapped her head to face the front of the schoolhouse.

That boy was trouble.

The very next day, Harvey stepped inside the schoolhouse door just as the final bell was rung. He removed his hat and hung it up on the wall peg. He put his lunch box on the shelf with all the other children's lunches. And suddenly, he was walking up the aisle on his hands. His legs waved in the air as he went. The whole class watched the spectacle, then burst out laughing as he turned right side up and sat in his desk with a goofy grin on his face.

Effie Kauffman giggled. Sam Stoltzfus laughed the hardest of all. Aaron Yoder was watching Harvey with a curious look on his face. If Lily didn't dislike Aaron so much, she would wonder what he was thinking. But she did dislike him, so she wasn't going to wonder what, if anything, might be on Aaron Yoder's mind. Probably, he was jealous that he had never thought of such a stunt.

Teacher Judith called the sixth grade history class up to the front of the room. "Watch this, Lily," Harvey whispered in his overly loud voice. He tucked his books under his suspenders and walked up to the front of the schoolhouse on his hands. Lily was astonished. That boy was brash.

"That's enough, Harvey," Teacher Judith said. "The first time was funny. The second time wasn't. I don't want you to walk on your hands during school hours."

Harvey flipped over to his feet and his books crashed on the floor. He picked them up and looked straight at Teacher Judith. "So you don't want me to use my hands during school hours."

"That's what I said," Teacher Judith said.

Harvey sat on the bench with the rest of his classmates. Lily returned to her own lessons and tried to ignore the lively history discussion of the sixth graders. An odd noise broke her concentration. She looked up to see the sixth graders returning to their desks. Harvey was kicking and pushing his books along on the floor in front of him.

"Harvey, pick up your books," Teacher Judith said.

Harvey gave her a flippant look. "Sorry. Can't. You told me not to use my hands during school hours."

Teacher Judith was losing patience, which was quite a feat. "I think you know what I meant."

Harvey grinned. "So I can use my hands after all?"

"Use your hands to take your books back to your desk," Teacher Judith said, slowly and clearly, as if Harvey might be very dim-witted.

Harvey picked up his books from the floor, slipped them under his suspenders, and walked back to his desk on his hands. Everyone burst out laughing again. Lily felt a little guilty about laughing, but it looked so funny! Then she caught Aaron frowning at her and her smile faded.

※

It didn't take Harvey Hershberger long to find his place in school. In fact, Lily thought he felt much too comfortable, too soon. From the first day on, Harvey made all the decisions about which games would be played at recess. He didn't want the first and second graders to play the same games as everyone else. "The little ones just slow everything down," Harvey insisted. In a way, it was true. But in another way, it wasn't very kind to exclude them. But Harvey wouldn't back down.

To Lily's shock, Aaron Yoder stood up to him. "I think we should let the younger grades play with us the way they always did." He scowled at Harvey. "The way they did before the Hershbergers moved in."

Sam Stoltzfus, who normally did anything Aaron Yoder did, sided with Harvey. "No! Harvey's right. It's high time those little children should play their own silly little games so the older grades can have more fun." The boys used up the entire recess arguing. Soon, Teacher Judith rang the bell and all the children had to run to the schoolhouse.

Lily had never heard so much fussing in the school yard before, even from Effie Kauffman.

September 28th

Dear Cousin Hannah,

It's been two weeks since you moved away and I still can't get used to it. I keep looking at your desk, expecting you to be there, but instead there sits a horrible boy named Harvey Hershberger. He is too horrible for words. A different kind of horrible than Aaron Yoder, but horrible all the same. Harvey likes to have everyone laugh at him, all the time. He can be funny, but he doesn't know when to stop and Teacher Judith is too soft on him.

I wish you still lived down the road and I wish you still went to school with me, but I do hope you like your new school. Write me soon and tell me all about the girls in your school. No boys, though. I've had my fill of boys.

Something interesting happened in school this week, if you want to call "trouble" interesting. It all started on Monday when Harvey Hershberger brought some long stick pretzels to school. During recess, the boys strutted around, pretending to be smoking them. It took a while for Teacher Judith to notice, and when she did, she didn't like it. But just as she started to scold them, they quickly ate those pretzels up. They acted like eating those pretzels was what they'd been doing all along.

On Wednesday, we were studying German spelling (you remember how boring that always was!). Harvey, Aaron, and Sam were whispering like thieves and suddenly, a funny smell, like burnt flour, came from behind me. When I turned around, I saw Harvey had lit his pretzel to smoke it. Aaron and Sam whispered to

Harvey to pass the matches. Soon, they all had smoking pretzels. It smelled awful.

Finally, Teacher Judith smelled it. She demanded that Harvey hand over the pretzels and the matches. All three boys had to stay in during recess, which was a relief to the rest of us. All except Effie. She thought Teacher Judith was being too hard on them (as if that were even possible!). She keeps making fun of Teacher Judith when she's sure the teacher can't hear her. Today, she imitated how Teacher Judith snores. If it's even partially true, I do feel a tiny little bit sorry for Effie's family. The snoring sound was awful, Hannah! Worse than a herd of pigs.

On Friday morning, all three members of the school board arrived at school. They made Harvey, Aaron, and Sam stand at the front of the schoolhouse while they gave a long lecture about the sinfulness of smoking. Then the boys had to apologize and promise they would behave from now on.

Fat chance of that!

Aaron, Sam, and Harvey laughed about getting in trouble during lunch recess, so I don't think they were very sorry at all. But I doubt they will try to smoke pretzels again.

Effie had said she wanted to try to smoke a pretzel, but changed her mind after the school board came calling.

Hannah, can you imagine how you would have felt if you had been scolded by the school board in front of the entire class? How awful!

You won't believe what Joseph's dog did last Saturday! I had been cleaning out my closet and found Sally (remember Sally? She was my rag doll). I put her on my *desk chair to play with her later, when I finished with the Saturday cleaning. Dozer must have sneaked into my room and grabbed her, because I found her out in the backyard, all chewed up. I was so mad! I yelled so loudly that Mama came running. He's a horrible dog, Dozer is.*

Mama is calling so I'd better close. Write soon, Hannah. Remember our promise to write every week. I'll try and do better. I want to hear all about your new home. I guess you could tell me about the boys in your school if you really have to.

Your cousin,
Lily

Who's the Next Bishop?

$\mathcal{L}$ily's back ached. She had been sitting on a hard, backless bench for hours. Today was Communion Sunday, which lasted all day long. Once it was over, there would be special services to ordain a bishop. Lily's church had been sharing a bishop with another district, and it was time to ordain one of their own.

The new bishop would be chosen from the three ministers in Lily's church: Effie's father, Henry Kauffman; Aaron's father, David Yoder; or Lily's Uncle Jacob. Lily gave some thought to the choice. She decided the new bishop would probably be David Yoder. Henry Kauffman might be the oldest, but he had a wife like Ida. No one in Cloverdale would ever want Ida Kauffman to be a bishop's wife! She would consider it her duty to spy on church members and inform her bishop husband about what people were doing wrong.

Actually, Lily thought, trying to stifle a grin, Ida Kauffman already did consider that to be her duty.

David Yoder would make a fine bishop for Cloverdale. He was a very kind man and his wife was very kind, too. It was a pity that Aaron Yoder was their son. Lily felt sorry for David Yoder and imagined that he was sorry about Aaron, too. But she did think he would be a good bishop. Uncle Jacob would be a good bishop, the best of all, but he was young. He had just become ordained as a minister last year.

Yes. Lily was confident that David Yoder would be the choice.

Henry Kauffman was preaching a very, very long sermon, and finally came to an end. Now would be the time for *Zeugnis*, when the other ministers shared their thoughts about the sermon the minister had finished preaching. Today, there were several benches filled with visiting ministers and bishops who wanted to witness the ordination. Lily swallowed a yawn. She knew it would take a long time for each to have a turn and share his thoughts. That was one thing she had learned about ministers: they were never shy to share their thoughts.

At long last, the closing hymn was announced and everyone started to sing in the familiar slow, rhythmic way. Lily's church sang the same hymns, in one voice, the same way all their great-great-grandparents used to sing.

Today, just once, Lily wished they could speed up the hymn. Wasn't anyone else eager to find out who the new bishop would be?

After the last hymn ended, everyone went outside to get some fresh air before it was time to head back inside. Lily joined the other girls in the kitchen who were waiting to get a drink of water. Effie was beside herself with excitement.

She was beaming, positively beaming. "I can't wait to see who the new bishop will be," she said. "Becoming a bishop's family means that family is the most important one in the community. My mother said so, just this morning."

Aunt Lizzie, Uncle Jacob's wife, would never say such a thing. Neither would David Yoder's wife. *Dear God,* Lily prayed silently, *please don't let the bishop be Effie's father. Please, please, please.* She didn't think she could stand Effie any more proud or puffed up than she already was.

Lily filled a glass with water and drank it as slowly as she could before it was time to head back into the room filled with benches. A visiting bishop cleared his throat and got slowly to his feet. His eyes swept the room filled with people. He looked kind and compassionate, almost as if he felt sad to ordain a new bishop today. "We all know why we have gathered back together this day," he said. "If all the visiting ministers and bishops would join me in the basement, we will be ready to start taking your votes."

Lily watched Henry Kauffman, David Yoder, and Uncle Jacob. They sat on the front bench, heads bowed, bearded chins to their chest. Lily wondered if they were all praying that God would let one of the other two ministers become the bishop. She almost giggled out loud. How could God answer such a prayer? If so, someone's prayer couldn't be granted.

All the men went down to the basement and lined up. One by one, they whispered their vote, their choice of whom they'd like to see as bishop, to one of the visiting ministers. After the last man sat down, it was the women's turn to vote. Afterward, everyone sat quietly, waiting. Waiting, waiting, waiting. It felt like a heavy silence. Lily didn't dare wiggle or move an inch. It almost seemed irreverent to breathe.

The sound of heavy feet on the basement steps broke the silence. The bishop led the way back to the front of the room. He carried three hymnals in his hands, each held shut with a rubber band. That meant all three of the ministers were chosen to be in the lot. Effie could hardly keep the smile off her face. She stretched and craned her neck to see the hymnals. Lily wanted to pinch her.

"The votes have been cast," the bishop said. "Now I ask Henry Kauffman, David Yoder, and Jacob Miller to come forward and take a hymnal."

One by one, the three men rose from the bench and chose a hymnal, then sat down again. The bishop read a few verses from the book of Acts in the Bible. It described how an apostle had been chosen, after Jesus had returned to heaven, to replace Judas Iscariot as the twelfth disciple. The bishop closed the Bible and read a prayer from the little black prayer book.

It was finally time.

Everyone leaned forward on the benches. The only sound in the room came as the bishop took the hymnal from David Yoder's hands and opened it. He paged through it and handed it back to him. Empty. Next he took the book from Henry Kauffman. Effie wiggled in her seat. The bishop paged through the hymnal and handed it back to Henry. Empty. Effie slumped.

There was only one hymnal left. The bishop took the hymnal from Uncle Jacob's hands and opened it. He held up a slip of paper for everyone to see. "The lot has been found," he said in a shaky, choked up voice. It almost sounded as if something terrible had happened. "God has chosen Jacob Miller to be our new bishop."

Aunt Lizzie started to cry. Other muffled sobs started around the room. The bishop placed his hands on Uncle Ja-

cob's head and prayed a prayer of blessing. Effie had stopped
wiggling and acted very bored.

Men and women rose from their seats to shake hands with
Uncle Jacob and Aunt Lizzie and to whisper words of en-
couragement to them. Lily wove her way through the crowd
to join the girls outside.

Effie squinted her eyes at Lily. "Jacob Miller took the book
that my father was supposed to get," she said in her peevish
way. "Jacob Miller doesn't have any idea about being a bishop.
His wife is too busy with little children to pay any attention
to the church members. She'll never make sure they're living
according to the Ordnung."

Lily stared at Effie. "Uncle Jacob did not take your father's
book! He took the last book. And I think he will make a

87

very good bishop. Aunt Lizzie will make a good bishop's wife. She's nice and not bossy and nosy like . . . some other people." Like . . . *your mother*!

Effie was furious. "My mother is one of the most valuable members of the church! She should be the bishop's wife! She'd be much better than your Aunt Lizzie!"

Lily opened her mouth to tell Effie just what she thought of Ida Kauffman when she felt Mama's firm hand on her shoulder. "Time for us to go home, Lily."

As Lily followed Mama to the buggy, she turned back to look at Effie. Effie squinted her mean little eyes at Lily, and Lily squinted right back.

On the way home, Lily couldn't help feeling a tiny bit smug. It would be nice to have her uncle for the bishop. Effie's father was only a minister. Maybe she would stop trying to boss Lily around, seeing as how Lily's uncle was the bishop.

And then she realized she was starting to think just like Effie.

A Talk with Mama

Every Saturday afternoon, Mama brushed out and washed Lily's long hair. It was awful! She dreaded it. Her hair reached below her waist now—it had never been cut—and it was always full of snarls. Lily felt like crying, but she was halfway to turning eleven. Too old to cry about tangled hair. But oh! how it hurt.

The only thing that helped to distract Lily was when Mama told her stories about her childhood. "Tell me a story, Mama," Lily said, wincing from the pain.

"I think you already know most of them by now," Mama said, gently combing out a section of Lily's hair. "Have I ever told you about the big snowball bush we used to have outside our house?"

"I don't think so," Lily said. She felt herself relax, ever so slightly, as she anticipated Mama's new story.

"When I was a little girl, I had a best friend named Dorcas.

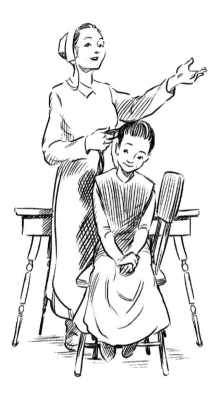

She lived right across the road from us. We sat beside each other in church and played together during every school recess. We used to spend time at each other's homes. Our favorite times were when we had permission to stay overnight." She pulled some tangles out of the comb and tossed them in the sink.

"One summer afternoon, we hatched a plan as we sat under a huge snowball bush at Dorcas's house. It was loaded with big white balls of flowers. Whenever we bumped it, it showered petals on the ground that looked like snow. Dorcas got a funny look on her face. She had an active imagination, and I knew she was thinking up something clever to do. Sure enough, she was brewing up an idea.

"'Let's gather up these flowers and shake the petals into a pail,' Dorcas said. 'On Sunday evening, as my sister and her boyfriend come home from the hymn singing, we could be waiting for them by the register in my room. It's right above the living room door. When they walk up to the door, we could dump the whole pail right on top of them.'

"I thought it sounded like a wonderful idea! All I needed to do was to convince my parents to let me stay at Dorcas's house for the night. I tried to pretend it was just an ordinary summer night, so they wouldn't suspect that we had something up our sleeves. But I was so excited when they said yes!

"On Sunday afternoon, Dorcas and I spent an hour plucking blossoms off and shaking the petals into a big five-gallon pail. When it was full, we made sure no one was looking as we sneaked it into the house and up to Dorcas's bedroom. When it was bedtime, we changed into our nightgowns and waited for her sister to get home. The time got later and later, but we didn't have much of a problem staying awake. There was always so much to talk about."

"Even though you saw each other every single day?" Lily asked.

"Even so. Just the way you and Hannah liked to talk to each other." Mama stroked the comb through Lily's hair one more time, looking for tangles, and found some.

Ouch! Lily winced.

"Dorcas and I sat on the floor to play games until we heard a horse and buggy drive into the driveway. We blew out the lamp and rolled the rug back to uncover the register. Dorcas carefully lifted it out. It left a square hole in the floor and we could see straight down into the living room. We tried not to giggle as we held the pail over the register, just waiting for them to come in the house."

By now, Lily had forgotten all about her tangled hair.

"The door opened and Dorcas's sister and her boyfriend walked inside. The boyfriend put his hat on the table while Dorcas took off her bonnet and hung it on the wall peg. We could hear them whisper to each other. They walked to the living room . . . and just as they passed beneath the hole in the floor, we dumped that pail of petals right down on top of them. They both looked up in surprise and saw us before we could duck away!"

Mama separated Lily's hair into three strands and started to make a braid. "Dorcas's sister was furious. She marched upstairs and told us to go downstairs and clean up the mess. It wasn't nearly as fun to clean up as it had been to dump the flower petals on them. After we were done, she sent Dorcas back upstairs and told me to go home." She tied off the ends of Lily's long braid.

"I ran across the road and tiptoed up the porch steps. I was hoping to get inside the house and up to my room without waking up my parents. I knew they wouldn't be very happy with what we'd done, and I hoped Dorcas's sister wasn't going to tattle. I turned the doorknob carefully, but it was locked. I didn't know what to do. I couldn't go back to Dorcas's house. If I woke up my parents, there would go my hope that they wouldn't find out what had happened. So I decided to sleep in the buggy in the barn. I curled up on the floor of the buggy under a buggy robe and tried to go to sleep."

"Wasn't it scary out in the barn?"

"It *was* scary!" Mama said. "Much scarier than I thought

it would be. The barn was pitch dark. The buggy smelled like a horse. And I kept hearing the animals move around in their stalls. I was cold and uncomfortable, and sure I would never sleep at all. But I must have finally fallen asleep because the next thing I knew, it was bright and sunny, and I heard the barn door open. My father was starting morning chores. Very carefully, I slipped out of the buggy and ran to the house. Somehow, my mother spotted me coming out of the barn. She opened the door as I tiptoed up the porch steps. So I had to tell her everything that had happened. If I'd known I was going to get caught, I would have just knocked on the door and slept in my comfortable bed all night instead of sleeping in a stiff buggy."

"Did you get in trouble?" Lily asked. It was hard to imagine Mama ever getting into trouble.

Mama twisted Lily's braid up into a bun and fastened it with several hairpins. "No, I think my parents decided that sleeping in a buggy had been punishment enough. Dorcas and I decided it was worth the trouble. For the rest of the summer, whenever we remembered the look on their faces when those petals showered down on them, we doubled over in fits of giggles." She pinned a cleaned, ironed prayer covering on Lily's clean, smooth hair. "Some things are just worth the trouble."

Some things definitely were, Lily agreed. But not combing out hair.

❦

Lily looked down at the English book spread out on her desk. Teacher Judith had told the fifth grade to do their next lesson but she hadn't explained how they were supposed to do it.

Lily tried to read the instructions again, but they made her feel even more confused and helpless. *Put parentheses around each prepositional phrase. Draw one line under the subject, two lines under the simple predicate, and three lines under every superlative.*

It was like reading another language!

Lily tried not to panic. From fourth grade, she remembered that a noun was a person, place, or thing. She tried to think back to other lessons that Teacher Rhoda had given. She felt pretty sure that a simple predicate was a verb but she didn't know what a superlative or a prepositional phrase was.

She used to like English. Teacher Rhoda had made it fun. She remembered an assignment that was especially easy: circling adjectives.

She could think up a lot of adjectives to describe her English lesson: *hard, awful, confusing, frustrating.* Teacher Rhoda would have been happy to know that Lily was thinking about adjectives, but that wouldn't help her with superlatives right now. What in the world was a superlative?

Lily raised her hand. Teacher Judith walked over to her desk to see what she needed. "What is a prepositional phrase and a superlative?" Lily asked.

"Read your instructions," Teacher Judith said and walked away to help someone else.

An odd thought dawned in Lily's mind. It almost seemed as if Teacher Judith didn't know English grammar. If that were true, what more could Lily do? Her only hope was to guess at the answers. She hoped she guessed enough right answers to get a passing grade.

❧

The next day, Lily walked home from school slowly, feeling ashamed. She didn't want to show her report card to Papa and Mama. Right in the middle of a row of As and Bs was a big fat F in English. She had never received an F before. Never! Why, she had never even had a C before. She wondered if F meant Failed. That's how it felt.

But then she cheered up. The problem wasn't her. The problem was that Teacher Judith didn't know English. Lily hoped Papa and Mama would understand how hard it was to figure out grammar when your teacher didn't know what it was.

Papa and Mama exchanged a concerned look when they saw the F in Lily's report card, but they didn't say anything more about it. At bedtime, Papa sent the boys upstairs and said, "Lily, we want to have a little talk before you go to bed."

Lily went into the living room and sat on a stool by the woodstove. Papa and Mama sat in their chairs. "Do you have any idea why you received an F in English?" Papa said. "You've always had As in English."

"I don't know how to do the lessons," Lily said. "Teacher Judith never explains how to do them. She just tells us to read the instructions, but I don't understand them. No one does. All of the upper grades failed. Beth and Malinda got Fs, too." She was sure Effie did, too, but Effie refused to show her report card to anyone.

"Everyone?" Papa said.

"Even Aaron Yoder got a D," Lily said. Everybody knew he always got the best grades in school.

Papa and Mama sat quietly for a few minutes. The only sound was the crackling of the fire in the stove. Finally, Mama said, "You can go to bed now, Lily. Papa and I will think of some ways we can help you."

Lily was relieved that Papa and Mama understood about Teacher Judith. She wondered what they would try to do about it. Maybe, they could take the report card to school and ask Teacher Judith to change the F to an A. That would be an excellent solution.

A few days later, Lily came home from school and found an English book waiting on the kitchen table for her. "Show me what lesson you're working on in school," Mama said.

Lily paged through the book until she came to the lesson she was supposed to do the next day. Mama looked at it and sat down next to Lily. She explained how to do all of it. When Mama helped her understand what the big words meant, Lily could understand it easily. She felt light and happy. She didn't dread school tomorrow. She was sure she could get a good grade with Mama as her teacher.

The next day, Teacher Judith assigned the fifth grade an English assignment. Lily pulled out her book and set right to work. It didn't take long to finish it. She was surprised how fun it had been to do her lesson now that she knew how to do it. Mama made everything so clear.

Each evening, Mama explained the next day's lesson to Lily. Her grades in English were back to As, while the rest of the upper grades were failing. Lily felt a little sorry for Beth and Malinda, but not Effie. It was a pity their mothers couldn't help them at home like Mama was doing for her.

❦

Dear Hannah,

Thank you for your letter. I'm glad your papa found a good hired boy to help him at the farm. Next time you write, tell me more about your new school. You didn't say if there were any girls in your grade. Only boys? If so, then I am doubly sorry for you.

Effie Kauffman made a big fool of herself over Aaron Yoder this week, same as every week. She is convinced that she will marry Aaron Yoder one day even though he doesn't like her at all. Last Friday afternoon, it was rainy and cold so we had to play in the basement for recess. The girls played hopscotch while the boys made up a game with the mop pails. They were trying to pitch tennis balls into them to score points.

When Teacher Judith rang the bell, Aaron Yoder opened the furnace door to see if it needed more coal. When he tried to close the door, Effie stuck a mop handle into the crack between the hinges. It got pinched in the door hard enough that it made a notch in the mop handle. Aaron opened the door and Effie took the mop out and kissed the notch on the handle. She said that mop was now hers to use whenever the schoolhouse needed cleaning, and it would help her to think of Aaron—as if she needed any reminding.

Aaron told her the only thing she kissed was a bunch of germs on a dirty mop. Naturally, Effie didn't care.

Isn't Effie ridiculous to be thinking about getting married? She acts like she is eighteen years old, not eleven.

When I grow up I want to live alone with a fluffy yellow cat for company. I want a little house, filled with books, that sits right next to an ice-cream store so I can read and eat ice-cream cones all day long. Doesn't that sound nice? Much nicer than getting married to a boy like Aaron Yoder.

I have some good news and some bad news. The bad

news first: Teacher Judith does not know how to teach English and the entire upper grades, except for one student who is getting an A, are failing.

Here is the good news: I am that one student.

Your cousin,
Lily

A Wedding

One afternoon in November, Papa brought the mail to Mama. On the top of the pile was a postcard. Mama read the postcard out loud so that everyone could hear. It was an invitation to a wedding for one of Uncle Ira's daughters.

Lily didn't even bother to ask if she could go to the wedding. Last year, Mama and Papa went to a relative's wedding and left Lily and Joseph at home with a babysitter. They thought going to school was more important than going to a wedding.

This year, Lily agreed with Mama and Papa. Teacher Judith promised a wonderful prize to the student who had the best attendance this school term. So far, Effie and Lily were the only students who hadn't missed a day of school. Effie pointed out, frequently, that Lily had missed the first two days of school because of her grandfather's funeral, but the school term had just begun. In a tiny corner of Lily's mind, she had a hope that Effie might end up with a bad cold or hacking cough once or twice and have to stay home. If that were to happen, Lily and Effie would be tied. Lily didn't want to risk her chance for the prize.

"Are you going to go?" Joseph said.

Mama looked up at Papa and smiled when he nodded. "Looks like we are," Mama said. "We'll take Dannie and Paul with us again. Maybe Carrie Kauffman might be able to come stay with the two of you."

Lily and Joseph exchanged a worried look. Last year's experience with Carrie as a babysitter was a disaster. Carrie didn't know how to milk Pansy. Poor Pansy! Lily and Joseph talked her into letting them eat raw, salted potatoes for supper and their tummies hurt for days. But the worst of all was when Joseph spilled green paint over his hair. Weeks later, his hair still had a strange greenish tinge. Lily grinned. She still remembered Ida Kauffman peering at Joseph's head during church and blinking rapidly, as if she couldn't believe her eyes.

"Carrie doesn't know how to milk a cow," Lily reminded Papa. She couldn't bear to hear Pansy's sad moos from an overly full udder. And she never did have as much milk as she did before Papa and Mama went to that wedding.

"That shouldn't be a problem," Papa said. "It's getting close to the time to dry Pansy off. I'll just let her dry off a month sooner than I planned. Chores won't be difficult this time. By the time we leave for the wedding, all you'll have to do is feed Pansy, Jim, and the goats. And gather the eggs."

Outside, Dozer chased a chicken until she flew up a fence, safely out of his reach. Papa should have added that they would have to keep an eye on Joseph's pesky dog and make sure he stayed out of trouble.

The evening before Mama and Papa planned to leave for Kentucky, Carrie Kauffman arrived with her battered brown suitcase. As long as she didn't have to worry about Pansy's milking, Lily was looking forward to Carrie's visit. She remembered how Carrie had played games with her and Joseph. Best of all, Carrie always did all the dishes. She never asked Lily to do them and Lily never volunteered.

Early the next morning, before dawn, Mama, Papa, Dannie, and Paul left for Kentucky. Lily didn't even hear them leave. Carrie, Lily, and Joseph headed out to the barn together to do the morning chores. It didn't take long to give Jim and Pansy scoops of grain and several slices of hay, and to make sure there was plenty of water in their troughs. Joseph took care of the goats and chickens. Inside, over a leisurely breakfast, Lily thought this time with Carrie was going well. Much, much better than last time, when Carrie's face often had a headachy look, and she had left Whispering Pines the moment Papa and Mama returned. So far, so good.

But when Lily returned from school, the house smelled awful! Carrie was nowhere to be seen. Lily peered into a bowl on the sink. It was full of burnt Grape-Nuts. She saw Carrie cross the yard from the barn with a little pail filled with eggs. "I did the chores so we can have an early supper," Carrie said. "I thought we could play some games this evening."

How wonderful! Lily ran upstairs to change into her play dress. She helped Carrie prepare supper by opening a can of applesauce. Lily was just about to pour it into a serving bowl, the way Mama did, when she had a better idea. Why give Carrie more dishes to wash? She stuck a spoon into the can and set it on the table. Carrie fried some hamburgers, and the three of them sat down to eat, much earlier than usual.

The smell of burnt Grape-Nuts lingered in the kitchen. Even Joseph noticed. "What stinks?" he said.

"I wanted to toast Grape-Nuts today," Carrie said. "When I was toasting them, one of my friends stopped in to say hello. I forgot that I had the Grape-Nuts in the oven until I smelled them burning. The next batch turned out well, though."

"Yum!" Joseph said, smacking his lips. "Grape-Nuts for breakfast are my favorite."

"So much better than porridge," Lily said.

"I'm not sure what to do with those burnt Grape-Nuts," Carrie said.

"Feed 'em to the goats," Joseph said. "They'll eat anything."

Like brothers, Lily thought.

Carrie's visit went so well that Lily didn't even miss Mama and Papa like she did last year. A little bit, but only at certain points of the day, like right as she went to sleep, or as she came home from school in the afternoon. It wasn't long before the visit came to an end and Mama and Papa returned. Carrie didn't seem to be in a hurry to get home like she did last year, either. She offered to help Mama unpack before she left for home, but Mama turned her down and hurried Carrie out the door.

It was unlike Mama to be brisk, but soon Lily found out why. "It was a lovely couple of days, until the last few hours," Mama said. Lily reached out for Paul but Mama didn't pass him to her like she normally would have. "Uncle Ira's youngest son broke out in chicken pox. That's the most contagious time for chicken pox. I'm afraid the boys were exposed."

Oh no! Lily and her brothers had never had chicken pox. If Dannie and Paul did get sick, that meant Lily would get sick, too. And that would mean she wouldn't be able to win the prize for best attendance at school! She had her heart set on winning that prize. She knew Effie was just as determined to win it, but it was only November.

"Mama and I discussed it on the way home from the wedding," Papa said. "We don't want to spread the chicken pox here in Cloverdale. Since it's likely that Dannie and Paul will get them, we won't be going anywhere until they're better. Lily and Joseph, we want you to stay at Grandpa and Grandma Miller's so you won't get them, either."

Mama packed a suitcase with Lily and Joseph's clothes. She filled a grocery bag with some of their favorite books and games. Lily felt excited and sad at the same time. It would be fun to stay with her grandparents, but she would miss Papa and Mama and her little brothers. She hoped Dannie and Paul would hurry up and get over the chicken pox fast so they could be a family again.

Papa hitched Jim to the buggy. He put the suitcases in the backseat. Mama gave Lily and Joseph a hug and told them to be good helpers for Grandma. Lily thought Mama looked as if she were blinking back tears. Lily's eyes started to sting. If Mama cried, Lily would surely cry.

Papa knew it was best to move things along. "Well, I think we're ready to go," he said. Joseph clambered up over the buggy wheel and hopped inside. Lily waited until Papa got Jim to turn the wheel out so she could use the buggy step to climb inside. It made her feel more grown-up to do it the same way Mama did. Papa lifted the reins and clucked giddyup to Jim. He trotted down the driveway. Lily waved goodbye to Mama and Dannie and Paul until they were out of sight.

Grandma Miller welcomed Lily and Joseph inside and took them upstairs to the guest rooms. She helped Lily and Joseph unpack their clothes and tuck them into dressers. Aunt Susie was delighted to hear they were going to live at her house for a while. She grabbed their lunch boxes and held them in the air. "I'll help Grandma fill these full of good things for you to eat at school tomorrow."

"But it's Friday night," Lily said. "We don't have to go to school until Monday."

Aunt Susie's face fell.

"Joseph and Lily will help you remember when it's Monday, Susie," Papa said. He was always especially kind to Aunt Susie, Papa was.

Aunt Susie's face crinkled into a smile.

Papa said goodbye to Lily and Joseph and started for home. Lily helped Grandma and Aunt Susie wash the rest of the supper dishes. Afterward, she helped Aunt Susie color in her coloring books. Being with Aunt Susie was like playing with a little girl. A grown-up little girl.

Bong, bong, bong . . . The big grandfather clock in the living room struck eight o'clock. Grandpa set aside the book he was reading. "I think it's time to go to bed." He reached for the little black prayer book on the stand beside his rocking chair. Everyone knelt while Grandpa read a prayer in his singsongy way. Lily's mind wandered off. She wondered what Papa and Mama and the little boys were doing at home. Papa was probably saying, "Bedtime for little lambs," and they would all climb into their own comfortable, familiar beds. Lily and Joseph would be sleeping in strange beds.

Lily climbed the stairs to the guest room. She slipped into her nightgown and got into bed. The mattress was hard and lumpy. It squeaked each time she moved. How could she ever sleep on a squeaky mattress? After tossing and turning for the longest while, she dragged all the covers off the bed and made a nest on the floor. She lay down and curled up. This was much more comfortable than the lumpy bed. No squeaking, either. All she could hear were the steady ticktocks from the grandfather clock in the living room. *Tick, tock, tick, tock.* The sounds echoed in the quiet house. Lily would never be able to fall asleep at Grandma's house. Not ever.

She turned over once more and it was morning.

The Chicken Pops

&ach day, when Lily and Joseph walked to school and home from school, they passed by Whispering Pines. In the mailbox, Mama would leave an envelope with instructions to help Lily with English class. Mama, Dannie, and Paul stood by the door of the house to wave to them as they passed. Papa came out of the workshop to wave to them. Dozer barked and danced around, but his collar was attached to a long rope so he couldn't follow them. It was the best part of Lily's day, even Dozer's silly dance. Lily was glad they could all see each other a little bit.

The following Sunday was a church morning. Lily jumped out of bed and hurried to get ready. She was sure she would see Mama at church. Mama never missed church. But at breakfast, Grandma Miller told her that they wouldn't be there. Mama and Papa stayed home with Dannie and Paul so no one else at church would get exposed to chicken pox. Lily was so disappointed. Church had never lasted so long.

In the afternoon, as they returned home, there was a box on the front porch of Grandma's house. She picked it up and carried it inside. After she opened it, she said, "I think this is for Lily and Joseph."

Lily peered inside. There was a bowl filled with Mama's oatmeal raisin cookies, a book Mama had been reading for bedtime stories before she had left for the wedding, and a fat envelope. The cookies looked delicious and the book would

be wonderful to read before bedtime tonight, but what Lily really wanted was the envelope. She tore it open as soon as Grandma handed it to her. Inside were letters from Papa and Mama. Dannie had drawn a picture. Another piece of paper had a tracing of Paul's little hand. At the bottom, Mama had written, "To Lily and Joseph. From Paul."

Tears pricked Lily's eyes and she blinked fast to keep them back. She unfolded the letter from Mama.

> *Dear Lily and Joseph,*
>
> *We all miss you so much and can't wait until you can come home. Dannie and Paul haven't shown any sign of the chicken pox. It will be two weeks on Wednesday since they were exposed to them. If they are still clear by the end of the week, then Papa and I think it will be safe for you to come home.*
>
> *Dannie has lost another tooth. He kept it so he can show it to you later. He has been trying to teach Dozer a new trick to surprise you when you come home but it hasn't been going very well. Dozer seems to miss you too. He lies down by the shop door and doesn't want to play. Even his favorite red ball doesn't hold his attention very long.*

Lily felt the tiniest pang of sympathy for Dozer, though it quickly left when she remembered how thoroughly he had chewed up her doll Sally. But she knew that Dozer just wanted everything to go back to normal. That's how she felt, too. She read on.

> *I have been busy sewing and mending. Paul wears out the patches on the knees of his pants as fast as I can*

*sew them on. Dannie has been trying to learn how to
sew patches too. So far he has managed to sew on one
patch. He still has trouble getting the thread tangled but
he is learning. If Dannie keeps on learning like this, Lily
might not have to do any more hand sewing.*

*We have been drinking goat milk regularly since Pansy
is dry.*

Lily felt like gagging. She hated goat milk. It tasted just
like a billy goat smelled: awful. That was the first good thing
she had discovered about not being at home. That and dis-
covering that Dannie was learning to sew. Two good things.

*I hope you're having fun at Grandma and Grandpa's
house. I'm sure Aunt Susie will be sorry when it's time
for you to come home.*

*Love,
Mama*

Lily flipped the paper over. Papa had written on the back.
His handwriting looked tall and handsome, just like him.

Dear Lily and Joseph,

*We miss having our family together. It will be very
nice once you can all come home again. The shop seems
lonely without Joseph making toys after school. I miss
Lily's cookies, too.*

He did? Joseph and Dannie gagged when they ate Lily's
cookies. That would be the first thing Lily would do when
she got home. Make cookies for Papa.

Last week, a couple came into the shop to order furniture. They brought their little boy along and forgot to watch him for a few minutes. In the blink of an eye, the little boy ran his hand along a tabletop that I had just finished putting a coat of varnish on. I had to redo the whole thing.

Lily could just imagine the scene. Papa wouldn't have been happy about the extra work the little boy had caused, but he wouldn't have said anything about it to the customers. He was *that* kind and understanding.

I've been getting a lot of orders for Christmas already. I hope I can get all of them done in time. It feels kind of nice to know Whispering Pines is helping to make Christmas special for folks.

How is everything going in school? I hope you are both doing your best. If you have any problems, you can always talk to Grandpa and Grandma. They will know how to help.

Love,
Papa

Lily handed the letter to Joseph to read and reached into the box to get a cookie. As delicious as Mama's oatmeal raisin cookie tasted, her stomach hurt as she ate it. She was even more homesick now than before she had read the letter.

❧

On Monday morning, Lily and Joseph looked at the windows of Whispering Pines as they passed the house, expecting to see Mama wave to them. But no one was at the window this morning. Papa didn't come out of his woodshop. It was the same thing in the afternoon. No one waved to them.

Aunt Susie was waiting for them on Grandma's porch steps. "Your papa stopped by today. Dannie and Paul have the chicken pops."

"Pox," Lily said sadly. "They have the chicken pox." She was so disappointed. She wasn't sure when she would ever get to go home.

"Why don't we make a busy book for Dannie and Paul," Grandma said. "It would give them something interesting to do as soon as they start feeling a little better. We can start it this evening after supper."

With that thought, Lily felt a little better.

After supper was over, Grandma slapped her palms on the kitchen table. "I think the ladies will let the men do the dishes tonight. We need to get started on that busy book."

Grandpa looked shocked. "Well, what do you think of that, Joseph?"

"I think it stinks," Joseph said, frowning.

Grandpa chuckled. "It never hurt a man to get his hands wet."

The two made a funny pair to watch. Joseph cleared the table, moving as slow as molasses in January. Grandpa was in a big hurry, filling the sink with warm water and stirring in soap to make it sudsy. Lily would have liked to watch them longer—it wasn't every day she saw Joseph or Grandpa wash a dish—but Grandma had disappeared off to her craft room.

Lily and Aunt Susie followed behind her. Grandma had spread out a pile of brightly colored felt on her craft table. She was digging through her pattern box. She pulled out an envelope that said BUSY BOOK in big black letters across the front.

Grandma handed Aunt Susie and Lily a sliver of bar soap to trace around the patterns onto the felt. A funny bumpy cloud-looking pattern was actually supposed to be the top of a tree. Lily placed it on a piece of green felt and carefully marked around it with her soap sliver. Then she cut it out. Grandma was cutting out little red felt apples. After they were done, Grandma found a long strip of Velcro and cut little bits off. One half of each bit was sewed to the green treetop and the other half to an apple. Aunt Susie cut out a brown felt bushel basket. Grandma sewed the tree to a piece of white fabric and the bushel basket on another piece. She had already made two pages for the busy book. Dannie and Paul would be able to pick all those apples off the tree and put them in the basket.

Lily grinned. This was going to be fun.

By bedtime, Grandma had made several pages. One had a tent with a zipper that could open and close. Inside the tent was a little embroidered bear. Another page had felt flowers to pick and put in a vase. And another had a coat with hooks and eyes to open and close.

Lily could hardly wait until tomorrow night. Grandma had said they would work on it some more. She was sure Dannie and Paul would love playing with this interesting book. And she was happy to tell Joseph that he would be doing dishes another night.

❦

The busy book was finished after a few nights. Grandpa took it over and dropped it off for Dannie and Paul. Then

Grandma started a scrapbook for the boys using old calendars. Some evenings, they played a Bible game. Everyone had a Bible in their laps. When Grandpa said a letter of the alphabet, everyone quickly tried to find a verse that started with the letter. Whoever found it first, read the verse. Then the last letter in that verse became the first letter for the new verse. Everyone raced to see who could find a new verse. It was always fun. Aunt Susie couldn't read very well but she could still hunt for verses. Then, Lily or Grandma would help her read her verse.

Two nights ago, they had played Dutch Blitz. Last evening, Grandpa had set up the train set that he had when he was a little boy. Although two more weeks had passed, Lily hardly missed home anymore. She felt so comfortable at Grandma and Grandpa Miller's. She even slept on the squeaky bed.

❦

One afternoon at school, Lily wondered what Grandma had planned for that night. She always seemed to have something fun in mind. Teacher Judith stood by her desk. "Put your books away for dismissal." The students scrambled to get ready to leave. They stood to sing the parting hymn, and then Teacher Judith dismissed them. As Lily put her sleeve through her coat, she heard a horse and buggy drive into the school yard. She looked out the window to see who had arrived. It was Papa, driving Jim! She jammed her bonnet on her head, stuck her hands in her mittens, and ran outside.

Papa had a big smile on his face. "How would you like to come home again?"

"I would like that just fine," Lily said. She practically leaped into the buggy. She wasn't worried about acting like a grown-up lady today. She was too happy to go home.

Joseph came flying out of the schoolhouse and jumped into the buggy, as if he had been expecting Papa all along. Papa clucked to Jim and they were on their way. "Are Dannie and Paul better now?" Lily asked.

"They still look a little funny from the pox," Papa said, "but they're no longer contagious. It's safe for you to come home."

Jim trotted all the way home. Lily didn't wait to help Papa unhitch Jim from the buggy. She jumped down and ran into the house. As soon as she crossed the threshold, she took a deep breath. The house smelled just the way Lily had remembered. Warm, cinnamony, soft and inviting. Like Mama. Dannie and Paul were sitting on the living room floor, playing with their farm animals. They jumped up and ran to meet Lily. She tried not to stare at them, but they looked disgusting. Their faces were blotchy with red spots. Mama came downstairs. She gave Lily and Joseph a big hug. "It's so good to be a family again," she said.

It was good, so good, to be home.

Papa Saves the Day

Lily wished she could press her nose against the kitchen window but she knew that would only mean she would have to wash it. She didn't want to create any more need to clean than was absolutely necessary.

Outside, the snow swirled and blew around the house and piled in drifts in front of the door. The snow was so thick that she couldn't even see the light from the lantern in the barn where Papa and the boys were doing evening chores.

She hoped the snow would stop soon. Papa had made arrangements for Mr. Tanner to come tomorrow evening to take the family to a little Amish store to Christmas shop. Lily and Joseph needed to buy some gifts for the gift exchange at school. Lily had been looking forward to shopping for more than a week, but it looked as if the snow might put an end to those plans.

She turned from the window. "Mama, what are we going to do if it keeps snowing? It would be terrible if we couldn't buy gifts and didn't have anything to give at the Christmas program."

Mama left the stove and joined Lily at the window. She looked up at the gray sky. "I don't think you have anything to worry about. The snowplows have plenty of time by tomorrow evening to clear the roads. And even if they don't, we can always figure out something else for gifts."

Lily wasn't convinced. She thought a potential disaster was in the making.

"This isn't that big of a snowstorm, Lily." Mama smiled and went back to the stove to stir a pan of frying potatoes. "I remember a storm back when your Papa and I were courting that took the prize for the biggest snowstorm."

Lily leaned her elbows on the counter and rested her chin in the palms of her hands. She loved hearing stories about Mama and Papa's courting days.

Mama turned down the burner and covered the pot full of potatoes with a lid. She picked out an onion from a bowl, set it on a wooden cutting board, and sliced it in half. "We had all gone to a neighboring church district one Sunday for church and planned to stay for the evening hymn singing. It had started to snow during church—those heavy kinds of flakes that clung to everything. There was hardly any wind so the snow started to pile up fast. We thought about starting for home, but decided to stay. Usually, those fat snowflakes mean there's a lot of water in the snow, and the temperature wasn't very cold. We thought the snowstorm wouldn't last very long." She pulled the papery skins off the onion and tossed them in the sink.

"But that evening, while we were singing, the snow picked up and the wind started to blow. Papa started to worry about the weather, so we left before the singing was over. We'd only gone a mile or two when Papa's horse lost a shoe and started to limp. Papa got out to lead the horse. We crept along, mile after mile. Finally, we stopped at someone's home to see if we could leave the horse there and borrow a horse to get home." While she was telling the story to Lily, she diced the onion into small pieces, then added them to the pan of potatoes. She added a pat of butter and stirred the onions and the potatoes to keep them from sticking to the pan.

"After we had switched horses, the snow was even deeper. All the way home, the poor horse had to walk right into the wind. By the time we reached home, we were nearly frozen. Papa unhitched the horse and put him in the barn while I hurried into the house. I made hot chocolate to warm him up before he started for home."

"Papa loves hot chocolate!" Lily said. "Maybe that's why."

Mama grinned. "After he left, I realized that it was the Sunday before his birthday, and I had forgotten to give him a gift."

"Did you give it to him later?"

"Yes, but I didn't see him again until the next Sunday." Mama salted the golden brown potatoes and scooped them onto a platter. "He said he liked it just as much as if I had given it to him the week before."

"What was it?"

"Papa still has it," Mama said. "I gave him the green horse blanket we use for Jim."

Lily knew that green blanket very well! It was Jim's favorite.

A blast of cold air blew in the house when Papa, Joseph, and Dannie burst through the door, eager for dinner. Lily looked out the window again. The snow didn't bother her quite as much now.

⚜

The next morning, Lily woke to find two feet of snow on the ground. All the roads were closed. Lily and Joseph dressed warmly and waded through the knee-deep snow. Each step, plowing a path to school, was hard work. Lily was glad to see smoke rise from the chimney as they neared the schoolhouse. She couldn't wait to get inside and warm up by the registers before Teacher Judith rang the bell.

Today was the last day to practice the Christmas program. After all the classes had completed arithmetic, Teacher Judith announced that the rest of the day would be spent rehearsing poems and verses. Lily had memorized her parts. Half-listening to everyone recite the pieces, she kept an eye out the window, hoping and praying to see a snowplow.

Right before school was dismissed, Lily heard a strange rumbling noise come up the road. The students craned their necks to see what was coming. It was a giant snowblower. It gobbled up the snow on the road and blew it into the fields. Aaron Yoder kept tipping his desk back, farther and farther, watching the snowblower. Suddenly, his desk flipped back and he crashed to the floor. He lay on his back with his feet sticking up in the air. His books were scattered all around him. He had a bewildered look on his face, as if he didn't know how he had ended up on the floor.

The entire class burst out laughing, including Lily. She

cherished it as a never-to-be-forgotten moment—it wasn't every day that Aaron Yoder looked silly.

Teacher Judith rushed to help Aaron turn over his desk and gather his books. She glanced up at the clock on the wall. "I think we can dismiss a little early today."

The students ran to get their coats before Teacher Judith could change her mind. Why, she was so flustered she didn't even remember the last hymn for the day! Lily was so happy about the snowplowed roads that she practically skipped all the way home. They would be able to go shopping for gifts tonight!

Mama fixed a simple supper of tomato soup and grilled cheese sandwiches so they could be ready to leave the minute Mr. Tanner drove into the driveway. The sun had just set by the time they were off on the shopping adventure in Mr. Tanner's blue station wagon. Lily's heart sang with happiness. The day was turning out better than she could have imagined. And then . . . Mr. Tanner drove to the narrow road that led to the little Amish store. The snowblower hadn't bothered to plow such a small road.

Papa blew out a puff of air. "Doesn't look like we'll be driving down this road."

Mr. Tanner turned his car around. "Where to now?"

"Most stores are closed by now," Papa said. "Let's stop at a grocery store so we can at least pick up some candy canes."

Lily was crushed. Candy canes? Those weren't special. She had been looking forward to getting to choose something pretty and unique at the store, and now she would have to settle for something boring and ordinary.

Papa ran into the grocery store and came back outside with

several boxes of candy canes. They had barely arrived back home when Papa said, "Bedtime for little lambs."

"So early?" Joseph asked.

"I've got a little work to do in the shop tonight," Papa said, shooing Joseph and Dannie up the stairs.

Lily could have cried. Going to bed early felt like a punishment on any day—but especially so after such a dismally disappointing evening.

As Lily lay in bed, she listened to the hum of the diesel engine in Papa's shop. She tried to think up excuses to stay home from school tomorrow. She'd rather skip the Christmas program than see the sneer on Effie Kauffman's face when she received Lily's candy cane. Effie would make some snippy remark about how poor Lily's family was.

Yes, Lily definitely had to come up with a good excuse to stay home tomorrow.

But then she remembered Teacher Judith's prize for best attendance by the end of the school term. Effie had stayed at home with the stomach flu for two days last week so now the girls were in an even tie for the prize. She just couldn't stay home. She turned over and punched the pillow, mad and sad at the snow.

The next morning, Joseph burst into Lily's room. "Come see what Papa made!"

Lily jumped out of bed and followed Joseph into the kitchen.

There on the kitchen table sat twenty-four beautiful wooden pencil holders, smooth like silk and polished like satin, with candy canes in each one.

Papa smiled shyly. "Candy canes just didn't seem like enough of a gift for Christmas. I stayed up last night and made these."

"Papa stayed up late," Mama said. "After midnight."

Lily felt tears prick her eyes. She should have known Papa would fix something special in his shop. He could fix anything. "Oh, thank you, Papa." She gave him a big hug.

She couldn't wait to give a pencil holder to all the children in school. Even Effie.

A Visitor on Christmas Eve

*L*ily helped Joseph and Dannie carry firewood until the wood box was piled high. They brought another stack in and piled it on the floor beside the wood box. Papa wouldn't have to carry in any wood tomorrow. Christmas Day could stay warm and cozy for Papa.

"I think there's enough wood to last for several days," Papa said as Lily unloaded another armload of wood on the floor. He sat at the kitchen table and cracked nuts from a big bowl. Mama was by the sink, finishing a few more preparations for tomorrow's dinner. Everything was almost ready for Christmas.

Lily hurried to get the book Mama had been reading to them before bedtime. Mama put the last dish for tomorrow in the refrigerator and sat down at the table. Dannie and Joseph ran to the table. Papa cracked a few almonds for everyone as Mama opened the book to the bookmark. She hadn't read more than a few pages when they heard an odd sound outside. Then a funny rap on the door.

Papa got up to see who was at the door. Mama kept reading, but Lily's ears were strained toward the hallway. Who had come to Whispering Pines on this dark, snowy night?

Papa stuck his head around the doorjamb. "There's a man on the porch whose car got stuck in the snow. He was trying to walk home but twisted his ankle. He asked if I could give him a ride. He says he lives just up the road so I'm going to use the big sled to give him a ride rather than harness up Jim."

Joseph jumped from the table. "Can I go with you?"

Papa looked at Mama and waited until she gave him a nod. "If you dress warmly you can come along," Papa said. "You can help me pull the sled."

Joseph grabbed his coat from the wall peg. Mama tied a scarf around his neck. Lily pressed her nose against the cold window and watched Papa and Joseph pull the man on the sled up the road. "Can I stay up until they get back?"

"That would be nice company for me," Mama said. "I'll tuck Dannie and Paul into bed and then I'll be right back."

"But I want to stay up, too," Dannie said.

"Tomorrow is Christmas, Dannie," Mama said. "You want to get plenty of sleep tonight so you won't have to take a nap tomorrow."

Satisfied, he ran upstairs to bed and was calling for Mama to tuck him in before she even left the kitchen. Now that was an example of how smart Mama was. Dannie hated naps. He never wanted to miss anything.

Lily tried to crack a few nuts while she waited for Mama. When Mama came downstairs after she tucked Dannie and Paul into bed, she sat at the table with Lily. She picked up a nutcracker and started to crack almonds. The only sounds in the kitchen were the gentle hiss of the gas lamp and the shells of the almonds cracking. Now and then, a whoosh of snow blew at the windows and Lily remembered Papa and Joseph, out in the cold. She hoped they would be home soon.

"How did you celebrate Christmas when you were a little girl?" Lily asked.

"Pretty much the way we celebrate now," Mama said. "Grandma made our favorite foods and we were given plenty of candy and snacks, and a few gifts. Grandma would knit a pair of mittens for each of us. Even if we knew we'd be getting mittens, it was always fun to see what color they would be. I always hoped for a pink pair, but that never happened. Grandma didn't think pink was practical." Mama reached out for another handful of almonds. "And then we would sing our favorite Christmas carols. Later in the day, we would get together with family for a big meal, just like we do now. Your Uncle Jacob always seemed to choose the biggest and best candies and snacks. Aunt Mary and I didn't think that was fair, so one year we decided to teach him a lesson."

Mama went to the woodstove and added a few sticks of wood to keep the fire going. Lily watched every move she made, eager to hear the rest of the story, but she knew Mama wanted the kitchen to be cozy and warm when Papa and Joseph came home.

Mama came back to the table and sat down. "We had made homemade candy bars. We made one a little longer than the rest and hid a watch chain in the middle of the filling before we dipped it in chocolate. On Christmas Day, we made sure that Jacob was served first. Of course, he chose the biggest

candy bar, just like we thought he would. We tried not to giggle as he took a big bite and chomped down on that chain.

"But then . . . he let out a terrible yelp! He had broken a tooth on the watch chain. He didn't eat much of anything for the rest of the day. Neither did Mary or I. We felt terrible. It hadn't occurred to us that something bad could happen."

That, Lily thought, was interesting. Mama was always pointing out to Lily to think, think, think, before she acted. But it was just as hard for Lily as it had been for Mama.

Lily was having trouble keeping her eyes open. She felt drowsy from the warmth radiating off the woodstove. The kitchen still had that cinnamony smell left over from baking Mama had done that afternoon. Christmas was such a wonderful time of year. Mama stifled a yawn and glanced at the clock. "It's almost midnight. I think I'll just leave a lamp in the kitchen for Papa and Joseph. We need to go to bed."

Lily went upstairs and looked out the window. The snowstorm had passed and the sky was cloudless. The moon shone brightly on the freshly fallen snow. There was no sign of Papa and Joseph. She hoped they would get home soon. She shivered and climbed into bed to snuggle under the covers.

By the time Lily woke up the next morning, the sun was streaming through her window. It took a moment for her eyes to adjust to the bright light. It was Christmas morning! And she had overslept. She dressed as fast as she could and hurried downstairs to help Mama make Christmas breakfast. Mama was frying bacon at the cookstove as Lily came into the kitchen. "Papa and Joseph didn't get home until 3:30," she said. "They're both still sleeping. Papa will tell us all about it at breakfast."

As the smell of Mama's crisp bacon floated through the house, Dannie and Paul woke up and galloped downstairs like two noisy colts, excited Christmas Day was here. Lily shushed them so they wouldn't wake up Papa and Joseph, but all of a sudden, Papa walked into the kitchen, dressed for the day. "Why, there's my little helpers," he said, as cheerful as ever. "I'm ready to head to the barn to start the chores. Who wants to help me?"

Dannie ran to get dressed, while Papa helped Paul into his coat and mittens. The basement door banged behind them as they started for the barn and Lily and Mama finished preparing breakfast.

Since it was so late in the morning, Mama decided not to make a huge Christmas breakfast like she usually did. Lily was a little disappointed but tried not to show it. The table still looked nice with fried eggs, crispy bacon, corn flakes, and an orange beside everyone's plate. And no porridge! Not on Christmas morning.

Joseph came downstairs, rubbing his eyes, as Papa and the younger boys came back in from the barn. They gathered around the table and had a moment of silent prayer. Papa slid an egg onto his plate. "Well, Joseph, you and I had quite the adventure last night, didn't we?"

Joseph nodded his head, but he was too busy eating to answer.

"We pulled the sled down the road, past a couple of houses," Papa said. "The man kept saying just a little farther, just a little farther. So we kept on going. When we reached the end of the road, he told me to turn left and keep going."

"Miles and miles and miles," Joseph added. He grabbed a handful of bacon from the platter. Mama reached out and held his wrist until he released most of the bacon.

Papa nodded. "We walked mile after mile before we finally reached his house. We helped him into his house and started for home. The snowplows hadn't cleared the roads yet, so when we climbed to the top of a hill, we would sit on the sled and fly down to the bottom."

"That part was fun," Joseph said around a mouth full of bacon.

Disgusting, Lily thought. Watching Joseph eat was just disgusting.

"We didn't get home until 3:30," Papa said. "Worn out and ready for bed."

"And cold, too," Joseph said.

Papa finished eating his eggs and started to peel his orange. "That man must be very lonely. He lives by himself, his house wasn't clean or warm. Nothing felt like Christmas. I thought it might be nice if we took him the food Mama has prepared. We always have such a huge feast at Grandpa and Grandma Miller's house. I'm sure no one will miss a little extra."

Lily would! She would definitely miss Mama's special meal. She'd been looking forward to that turkey casserole, the special Christmas pudding, the angel food cake that had green and red Jell-O swirls in it. She was just about to say so when Papa silenced her with a look.

"Christmas is a time to reach out to others," Papa said, "the way Jesus reached out to us."

Mama packed up the meal she had prepared, including a basket of dinner rolls. Lily tried not to feel selfish, but she was mad at that man. Because of him, Papa and Joseph spent most of Christmas Eve pulling a sled in the snow. And because of him, they wouldn't be having Mama's special meal.

Papa, Joseph, and Dannie hitched up Jim to the buggy and dropped the meal off at the man's house. Mama, Lily, and Paul waited at the house for them to return before they all went to Grandma and Grandpa Miller's. When they returned, Lily scrambled in the back of the buggy and sat between Joseph and Dannie. "Did the man seem happy about the dinner?" Lily whispered to Joseph.

"Not really," Joseph whispered back.

"Did he say thank you?"

"No. He just took it."

Papa overheard. He pulled the buggy to the side of the road and turned to face Lily. "We didn't take Mama's good meal to the man so that he would thank us. We wanted to share a Christmas blessing with him."

"Yes, Papa," Lily said in a small voice.

"And one thing I promise you. Whatever you give to others, you will never miss."

Lily still wasn't sure. She was sorely missing the thought of that Christmas pudding. Mama made it only once a year. But she did appreciate her papa's tender heart.

A few hours later, Lily's tummy was stuffed. She had eaten more for Christmas lunch than ever before. Grandma offered her a bite of homemade fudge, and she had to turn it down. She couldn't eat another bite. Grandma smiled and bent down to whisper to Lily. "Your parents did the right thing to share their Christmas dinner. I have to admit that I missed your mama's Christmas pudding, but isn't it nice that someone else got to enjoy it?"

Lily hoped the man did, indeed, enjoy it.

The strangest thing was that everyone in Lily's big family ate their fill and then some at Grandma Miller's, yet there were more leftovers to take home than ever before. Papa said it almost seemed like a miracle. A Christmas miracle.

The School Board
Comes Calling
at Whispering Pines

ily looked out the kitchen window and saw three buggies drive up to the hitching rack by the barn. The three members of the school board climbed out of their buggies and tied their horses, looking serious and solemn. Papa walked out from his shop to meet them.

Lily tried to think of everything Joseph had done in school recently that might have gotten him into serious trouble, but she couldn't think of a thing. Harvey was the one who was constantly causing trouble. Then Lily's stomach did a flip-flop. She was the only one in the upper grades who was passing English. What if the school board thought she was cheating?

After a few minutes, Papa came to the house to find Mama.

130

She was feeding Paul in the kitchen. "Rachel, there are some folks here who want to talk to us."

Oh, boy. Something must be really wrong if they needed to talk to *both* Mama and Papa.

Mama looked at him curiously. "Lily, please finish feeding Paul for me." She handed Lily a bowl of peas, grabbed her shawl, and followed Papa outside. Lily's stomach clenched even tighter. She had a terrible feeling that something awful was coming, like the way the wind settled right before a storm hit.

Lily sprinkled peas on Paul's high chair tray. It was high time that little boy learned to feed himself. She opened the window a big crack to try to overhear the school board members. They were down by the buggies but their voices were too low and she couldn't understand what they were saying. All she could hear was the murmur of deep male voices. Mama wasn't talking at all.

After a long time, she saw Mama turn and head back to the house. Lily hurried over to resume feeding Paul. Instead of eating the peas, he had mashed them up with his fat little hands and made a green, mushy mess. Mama came into the kitchen so preoccupied she didn't even comment on Paul's green glop. "Thank you for taking care of Paul for me while I was outside," she told Lily. She didn't say anything about what the school board had wanted. She just picked up the spoon and started to feed Paul again.

Lily waited and waited, until she couldn't stand it any longer. "What did they want?" she asked. "Am I in trouble? Is Joseph?"

Mama looked up at her in surprise, as if she had forgotten Lily was standing beside her. "You and Joseph don't have to worry about anything."

Lily stayed right there, hoping that Mama would tell her why the school board had come calling, but Mama didn't say another word about it. Lily knew enough to know there was no point in asking her.

A few days later, the three members of the school board drove up to Whispering Pines again and parked their buggies. Again, Papa came inside and asked Mama to go down to the shop to talk to them. And again, Mama didn't say a word about what the school board had wanted. Over the next two weeks, the school board came two more times to have a talk with Mama and Papa. Then, they came for a fifth time with Uncle Jacob, the new bishop. *Oh, boy.* When the bishop arrived unexpectedly, even if he was Mama's little brother, something serious was up.

That evening, Papa and Mama told Lily and Joseph and Dannie that they needed to have a family discussion. Papa scooped Paul up into his arms and led the way into the living room.

Lily, Joseph, and Dannie followed Papa and Mama into the living room and sat on the couch facing them. What was going on?

Papa cleared his throat. "How would you children like a new English teacher?"

So that's why the school board came to visit! They wanted to get rid of Teacher Judith. In a way, Lily wasn't entirely surprised. Teacher Judith had terrible trouble keeping order in the class. The boys were constantly cutting up and creating disruptions. She never stopped them or scolded them or kept them after school. It was probably best that she be fired. "Where will Teacher Judith go?"

"She's still going to be your teacher," Papa said. "The school board is concerned about how she teaches English, so they have decided to hire a teacher to come in a few afternoons each week and teach English class."

"Who will it be?" Joseph asked.

"That's the best part," Papa said. He was beaming, positively beaming. "Mama has agreed to teach English two afternoons a week."

Mama? Mama would teach at the school? Lily was horrified! Mama might be good at explaining English so that Lily knew how to do it in school, but she didn't want her to *come* to school. Lily didn't want to share her with a schoolhouse filled with other children. She wanted to be in school and know that Mama was at home cooking, baking, sewing, and doing all the things that other mothers were doing.

Lily wanted things to stay the same, with Mama tutoring her at home so she got better grades than everybody else. Better than Effie and Aaron's grades. She liked being smarter than everyone else in school. In fact, she loved it.

What would happen when Harvey caused mischief? Or Aaron or Sam? Teacher Judith never knew how to handle mischief because it always came in a different form. Mama was so kind and never lost her temper. Why, Harvey Hershberger could run circles around her.

And what if Effie said mean things about Mama, or mocked her behind her back, the way she made fun of Teacher Judith? That was a very real possibility. She couldn't bear it if Mama were mocked by Effie.

Lily jumped up from the couch, ran up the stairs, and flopped on her bed. She buried her face in her pillow. Before she had a chance to start crying, she heard Papa's footsteps on the stairs.

Lily's door creaked open and Papa sat next to her on the bed. "Would you like to tell me why you're upset about Mama teaching English?"

Lily didn't want to tell Papa all the crazy thoughts that were running through her head. She couldn't even look at Papa. She shook her head and kept her face buried in her pillow.

In a gentle voice, Papa said, "Lily, sit up and tell me about it."

Lily sat up slowly. "I just don't want Mama to be the teacher."

"But why not?"

Papa gave her a moment to gather her thoughts. When Lily didn't say anything more, he tried to help her figure out what was wrong. "Are you afraid Mama won't know how to teach?"

Lily shook her head. That wasn't it. She was sure Mama would know how to teach. She knew most everything.

Papa finally gave up. "Lily, Mama needs our love and support right now. We're all going to work together to make everything as easy for her as we can. We will all need to pitch in and help more around the house while she studies and prepares lessons for school." He walked to the door, then turned back. "You might be surprised at how much you enjoy having Mama as a teacher. I have a feeling that the days she comes to teach might be your favorite school days of all." He closed the door as he left the room.

Maybe Papa was right. Maybe the whole situation would be better than Lily thought.

But then her thoughts traveled to Effie and Harvey. She lay there for the rest of the night, without a sigh left in her.

❧

Lily sat at her desk in school, anxiously looking up at the clock. Only fifteen more minutes before noon recess. During lunch, Mama would arrive at the schoolhouse and become the new English teacher. Lily had all kinds of feelings: nervousness, worry, and the tiniest little bit of excitement. She wondered what Papa would do to keep Dannie and Paul out of trouble. They liked to watch him work in the shop, but often he would shoo them upstairs to Mama because they were tempted to get too close to the machinery. Lily hoped Papa wouldn't use any noisy, dangerous machinery with Dannie and Paul nearby.

"Put your books away for recess," Teacher Judith said.

Desk lids clattered open and shut as books were shoved inside. When the students were ready, Teacher Judith told them all to stand.

The children rose and stood beside their desks to sing a little song to thank God for their food. Then they lined up to wash their hands at the sink and fetch their lunch boxes off the shelf. Lily was halfway through her sandwich when she heard a clopping of hooves and a jangle of harness. Her stomach did a funny little flip-flop as she looked out the window and saw Jim pulling the buggy. Papa stopped Jim in front of the schoolhouse and Mama climbed out of the buggy. Lily watched her wave goodbye to Papa, Dannie, and Paul before she came into the schoolhouse.

Teacher Judith welcomed Mama in. "I'll turn the schoolhouse over to you," she said. "I have a dentist appointment this afternoon, so I'll be leaving right away." Mama seemed a little surprised by that. The school board had wanted Teacher Judith to stay and learn from Mama along with the students so she could teach English on her own.

Mama walked to the front of the schoolhouse and placed her satchel on the teacher's desk. On a typical day, the children finished their lunches and rushed outside to play. Today, there was an exciting game of Prisoner's Base that had been carried over from morning recess and needed to be finished. But no one left the room. Even the big boys stuck around. Everyone was curious about the new teacher. Lily felt awkward. As she watched Mama get settled at the desk, she didn't look like Lily's mama. She looked like a teacher. It was an odd feeling. Lily wanted to run up to her and talk to her or help her. But at the same time, she didn't.

Finally, the children wandered out to the playground and picked up the game of Prisoner's Base. Soon, Mama rang the bell and recess was over. She told the students to continue working on their assignments. She would call each class, one at a time, to the front of the schoolhouse for English class. She started with the eighth graders. A rustling sound of papers shuffling and books opening rippled through the schoolhouse as the other classes got to work. Lily could hardly concentrate on her work as she watched Mama explain English to the eighth graders. Then it was the seventh graders' turn. Finally, Mama said, "Sixth grade, please come to the front."

The sixth graders hurried to the front of the room, all except Harvey Hershberger. He flipped over and started walking up the aisle on his hands. The schoolhouse was absolutely still, as if the children were holding their breath, watching Harvey and wondering how Mama was going to react.

This was *just* the sort of thing Lily had been dreading! Poor Mama. She was even sweeter and kinder than Teacher Judith. Harvey needed a teacher who would punish him and keep him after school and send scolding notes home to his parents. Lily was mortified for Mama.

Mama watched Harvey walk upside down to the front

row. She didn't look amused, but she didn't look flustered or upset. Lily couldn't tell what she was thinking.

After Harvey turned right side up and sat on the bench, Mama walked up to him. *Oh, boy. Here it comes.* Harvey would say something sassy to Mama, like he always did to Teacher Judith. Lily hoped Mama would punish him. *Scold him, Mama! Send him home!*

"Why, Harvey," Mama said, "that was quite impressive. You're very good at walking on your hands. Would you like to teach the other boys how to walk on their hands during next recess? I think most of them would like to know how. I can't think of a better teacher than you."

Harvey sat up so straight and proud that it looked like he had a ruler down his shirt back. "Well, I believe I could do that."

Mama nodded and turned her attention to teaching the English lesson to the sixth grade. Lily felt her face flame with embarrassment. It was clear that Mama wasn't going to be any stricter with Harvey than Teacher Judith. He would be running this classroom before long.

At recess, Mama reminded Harvey that he'd agreed to teach the boys how to walk on their hands. She told the girls that they could stay and watch if they wanted to or go outside to play.

Lily wanted to go outside and run away as far as she could. Poor Mama. She was giving Harvey all the attention he craved. He would be even more impossible to be around, and that would only encourage Aaron Yoder and Sam Stoltzfus to act up. Poor, poor Mama. She didn't know what she was in for.

None of the girls would go outside with Lily. They wanted to stay inside and watch Harvey. He worked up a sweat as he circled the room by walking on his hands, yelling out instructions right and left to the boys as he passed by them.

It was a cold winter day that brought a chill into the school-house, but by the end of recess the boys were exhausted, hot, and sweaty. Especially Harvey. He was silent for the rest of the afternoon, which was quite, quite unusual. Several times, Lily caught him rubbing his arms as if they ached.

Lily never saw Harvey walk on his hands again.

❦

Dear Hannah,

Thank you for writing and telling me all about the new hired boy at your farm. I'm glad your father chose someone big and strong. And cute, you said, though I'm not sure what cuteness has to do with working on a farm.

So much has happened in Cloverdale that I don't even know where to begin. First, here's a story you'll enjoy about our very own relatives:

Since our Uncle Jacob is the new bishop, Cousin Noah has been sitting on the preacher's bench, right up front. This morning, Noah was playing with his handkerchief. He wadded it up in a ball and popped it in his mouth (don't ask me why! boys do strange things like that) and then he started to choke! Uncle Jacob stopped preaching mid-sermon to take care of him, and then continued preaching like nothing had happened. On the way home, Papa said that Uncle Jacob was born for the bishop job.

During lunch on Friday, Aaron Yoder offered Wall-Eyed Walter five cents to eat a cup of sand in school. That was downright mean—everybody knows that Wall-Eyed Walter isn't the brightest lantern in the barn. Of course, he accepted Aaron's challenge. He took one bite and spit it out. All afternoon, he kept spitting and coughing and gagging. Teacher Judith finally sent him home.

Mama started teaching English twice a week—on Tuesday and Thursday afternoons. The school board kept coming to Whispering Pines to ask her to teach and she kept saying no, but then Uncle Jacob came with them to ask. I guess you don't say no to a bishop, even if he is your brother. She's doing a fine job. She has a clever way of taking the shine off Harvey Hershberger. Harvey has a disgusting habit of sticking his pen cap on the tip of his tongue and flicking it in and out of his mouth. On Thursday, Mama told the whole class that we were fortunate to have a rare blue-tongued boy in school. Just as unusual, she said, as the rare blue-footed chicken. After that, Harvey stopped sticking the pen cap in his mouth.

Lately all Joseph talks about is playing in the woods. He says he wants to live off the land like Teaskoota, the old Shawnee Indian who lives up in the hills in a little log cabin. If you ask me, I think Joseph is just trying to imitate Aaron Yoder (ridiculous! just ridiculous). Aaron is always traipsing off to the woods to fish or hike. Yesterday, Joseph disappeared to play in the woods. He saw a chipmunk and thought it would make a good pet. He waited, still as a stone, until it came near him. Then he reached out and grabbed its tail. The chipmunk scrambled to escape and its tail came off in Joseph's hand! Joseph felt horrible.

Your cousin,
Lily

Beth and the House Fire

*L*ily woke with a start. Something was wrong. The sharp whoop of a siren rushed past Whispering Pines—first one, then another. She shivered. Sirens made such an eerie sound, especially so in the middle of the night. She turtled her head down into her covers and wondered where the fire engines were hurrying to. Had there been an accident? The roads were icy. Sometimes cars slid into ditches. Or maybe there was a house fire. Lily burrowed down deeper under her covers. How awful it would be to be awakened by a fire in the middle of a dark, cold winter night.

During breakfast, someone rapped on the door. Papa left the table to see who had arrived, and he returned with David Yoder. Mama jumped up to get David a cup of coffee. "Thank you, Rachel," David said, putting his cold hands around the mug. "I came to let you know that Jonas Raber's house burned to the ground last night."

"Was anyone hurt?" Mama said, first thing.

"No," David said. "The family got out of the house in time, but they lost most everything. Everyone is gathering today to help with the cleanup."

Lily looked down at her fried egg. So that's where the fire truck was rushing to last night. Poor Beth! What a frightening experience it must have been—to watch your house burn down. How ghastly. What would the Raber family do without a house to live in? Lily put down her fork. She couldn't eat another bite of her egg.

David Yoder gulped down the rest of his coffee and left to go tell a few more families about the work frolic for the Rabers. Papa finished his breakfast, grabbed his hat and coat, and hurried outside to hitch Jim to the buggy. No work in the woodshop would go on today. Papa would spend the day helping the Rabers.

Lily cleared the table and went upstairs to change her clothes for school. She wondered if Beth would even be at school today. What did you say to someone whose house burned down? Lily didn't want to make her feel worse. Maybe Beth wouldn't want to talk about it at all. Or maybe, if Lily didn't ask her about it, Beth would think Lily didn't care. Lily didn't know what to say or not say.

As Lily put her bonnet on, Mama handed her the lunch box and said, "Good friends lend listening ears. I think you'll make a good listener."

It was astonishing how Mama seemed to know exactly what Lily was fretting over. "But what if Beth doesn't want to talk?"

Mama tied the ribbons under Lily's chin. "I think you'll be able to tell if Beth wants to talk or not."

When Lily arrived at school, she saw Beth standing by a window, a look on her face like she was staring without seeing anything. Lily removed her shawl and bonnet and hung them on a hook. Slowly she walked across the room. As she drew closer to Beth, she caught a whiff of a smoky smell. Beth was wearing someone's borrowed clothes and she looked exhausted, like she hadn't slept at all—her eyes were puffy from crying. Her face had a squinched-up expression.

"Are you all right?" Lily asked in a hushed voice.

Beth shook her head, tears starting all over again. "Lily, it was terrible! The fire was everywhere! It happened so fast. My brother Rueben ran over to the neighbor to call the fire trucks while Papa dumped water on the fire. Mama and I grabbed things and ran out of the house until Papa said we had to stay outside so we wouldn't get hurt."

Lily rubbed circles on Beth's back, hoping to comfort her. She was trying to be a good listener.

"It took the fire truck such a long time to get there," Beth said. "By the time it arrived, the house had collapsed in a heap. The firemen sprayed water on what was left of the house until the fire was completely out. A fireman carried me to his truck and let me sit inside where it was warm. I hadn't even realized I was standing in the snow in my bare feet."

Lily looked down at Beth's feet. She was wearing boots that were much too big for her.

"These are my cousin's old shoes." She tugged on her dress sleeve. "And her clothes, too. All my clothes were burned up."

Lily couldn't imagine what it must be like to have everything you cared about . . . gone. Just like that. She thought of her scrapbooks and her circle letters and the letters from Hannah that she kept in a special box. The closest she could get to imagining such loss was how she felt after Dozer chewed up Sally. Beth must be feeling one hundred times as bad.

Beth wiped away her tears with her dress sleeve. "By the time the fire truck left, there was nothing but ashes. We saved a few things, like Mama's sewing machine and a few pieces of clothing. Some dishes, too." She gave a little half laugh. "I was so scared that I saved the stupidest things."

"Like what?" Lily asked.

"I carried out the trash can and a box of onions," Beth said. Then her face crumpled into tears and she covered it with her hands. "But I forgot all about Pete!"

Oh no. Pete was a beautiful blue parakeet that lived in a pretty cage in Beth's living room. Lily knew how fond Beth was of Pete. She had even taught him a few words. To think Beth had saved the trash can and not Pete. How awful! She must have been in a dreadful panic to forget her special pet.

Would Lily remember Dozer if a fire swept through Whispering Pines? She hoped so, but after he had recently chewed up one of her favorite books, she wasn't quite sure.

⁂

After school, Lily helped Mama prepare stew for supper. "Lily, please go down to the basement and get some carrots," Mama said. Lily wrinkled her nose. That could only mean that Mama was going to put carrots in the stew. Lily loved raw carrots but it was another thing entirely to eat a cooked carrot. They became mushy and squishy and disgusting. She took a bowl and went down to the basement. Mama kept the carrots in a barrel filled with cold sand so they stayed fresh. Lily dug through the sand until she grabbed half a dozen carrots.

Lily washed and peeled carrots at the kitchen sink. She looked up and saw Jim pull Papa's buggy into the driveway. She hurried to cut up the carrots and plop them into the simmering pot of hamburger, onions, and cut potatoes. She wanted to hear everything Papa had to say about cleaning up the Rabers' house.

Instead of going to the barn, Papa drove Jim right up to the house. Through the kitchen window, Lily saw Beth jump out of the buggy. She dropped the last carrot in the stew pot and ran to the door. "Beth! Come in!"

Beth held up a rumpled brown paper bag. "Your father said it would be okay for me to sleep here until we get our new house."

Mama had come to the door when she heard Beth's voice. "You're more than welcome," she said. "Lily will be happy to share her room with you."

How exciting! Now Lily wished they could have prepared a delicious supper since Beth was here. Her friend had enough things going wrong in her life without having to eat carrot-filled stew.

Later that night, as the girls settled down to sleep in Lily's bedroom, Lily heard Beth start to sniff as if she was getting a cold. She popped up from her nest bed on the floor. "Do you need a handkerchief?"

When Beth turned to her, she burst into tears. "Oh Lily . . . it's all my fault," she sobbed.

Lily jumped up on the bed to sit next to her. "What is?"

"The fire! I burned down our house last night."

"But . . . how? Why would you do such a thing?"

Beth wiped her tears. "I didn't do it on purpose. As I was getting ready for bed, I lit my lamp, just like I always do. I shook the match to put it out, and the match head dropped and rolled under my dresser. I tried to look for it but couldn't find it. I figured it had just gone out. So I got back in bed and wrote in my diary, just like I always do. Then I got sleepy and went to bed. Not much later, I woke up and smelled smoke. The match head hadn't gone out and my dresser had caught on fire. Flames were licking at the walls. I jumped out of bed and ran down the hall, screaming to my parents and my brother to wake up because the house was burning down."

"Why didn't you tell your parents about the match head?"

"I couldn't! There was so much confusion going on, and since then, I haven't had a chance." She hung her head. "Plus, I don't know how."

"In the morning, let's ask Papa," Lily said. "He'll know how to help."

It was still dark when Beth woke Lily. She had heard Papa's footsteps go down the stairs. He was heading to the barn to do chores. Lily yawned and stretched, wondering if Beth had slept much at all. "Let's go talk to Papa," Lily said, grabbing a flashlight. "You'll feel so much better afterward." She knew that from personal experience. Trying to keep a secret from parents took a toll.

The two girls tiptoed down the stairs and out to the barn. When Lily pulled the barn door open, Papa looked up in surprise. He had just started to feed Pansy. The big cow turned and looked at Lily and Beth, blinking and batting her big, thick eyelashes as if to ask why the girls were up so early, then she turned back to her trough, deciding the hay was more interesting.

Lily grasped Beth's hand firmly and walked over to Papa. "Beth has something she needs to tell you."

Papa kept tossing fistfuls of hay to Pansy, as if this was the most ordinary way to pass the time—feeding a cow by lantern light with two little girls in their nightgowns. Lily squeezed Beth's hand.

"I burned my house down." Beth's voice was very small, almost a whisper.

Papa's expression revealed that he had not anticipated an announcement of that sort. "Go on."

"I didn't mean to," Beth said. "I lit a match and it dropped under the dresser. I did look for it but couldn't find it. Next thing I knew . . ." She threw her hands up in the air. "Whoosh! The whole house was burning down." Beth gave Papa all the details, every one, because once she got started, she wanted to get it all out.

Papa kept on putting hay in Pansy's trough, nodding in all the right places to Beth's story. When there was no more hay to toss, he walked over and put a hand on Beth's shoulder. "That's a very big burden for a little girl to carry, Beth. It was an accident. Accidents happen, all the time. No one will blame you, but keeping it a secret wasn't the right thing to do. Even if you didn't lie about it, you didn't tell the truth, either. It's always best to tell the truth. After school today, I'll go with you over to where your parents are staying and you can tell them the story for yourself." He picked up the lantern. "I'm sure they'll understand. Don't you worry yourself about it anymore." As Papa walked to the feed room, the swinging lantern cast eerie shadows on the walls.

As the girls went back to the house, Beth, Lily noticed, didn't have that squinched-up expression any longer.

Papa had answers for everything.

CHAPTER

17

Lily Has an Almost-Sister

*L*ily and Beth were eating their after-school snack at the kitchen table. Mama mentioned how low they were on bread for school lunches and started to pull out ingredients for bread making. Watching her, Lily hatched an idea. Papa had said to look for ways to help Mama while she was a part-time English teacher. "Can Beth and I bake bread all by ourselves?" she asked Mama. She looked at Beth and got a big smile in return. "We think we know how."

Mama's face was a mix of *That sounds like more work than help* and *Why not?* The *Why not?* won. "I suppose you could give it a try. It would give me time to get some other things done this afternoon. I was going to make four loaves, so if you need help with measuring ingredients, just ask me."

How hard could it be? Lily had watched Mama make bread dozens of times. Making bread was easy. One cup of warm water, one teaspoon salt, one tablespoon sugar, and one tablespoon of butter for every loaf of bread. Easy. Today she would need four of each. And Beth could help with counting so they wouldn't mix anything up. Beth was excellent at math. Just excellent.

Mama went upstairs with baby Paul, and the girls got right to work on baking bread. After the butter had melted into the warm water, it was time to add the flour. One cup of flour for every loaf. Lily carefully measured two cups of flour into the bowl as Beth mixed. Then Lily sprinkled another cup of flour on top and Beth mixed it in. Then another. They counted each cup out loud so they wouldn't mix anything up. As soon as the dough became too stiff to be stirred with

a wooden spoon, it was time to knead it. Now the fun part could begin.

Lily and Beth punched their fists into the dough, lifted it, turned it, then punched some more. They pretended the dough was the boys' faces in the upper grades and punched down with even more vigor. It was still sticky, so they added more flour. They kept on punching and adding flour until they had a nice big ball of bread dough that was no longer sticky.

Lily covered the bowl with a kitchen towel. She set the bowl in the warm corner of the sink beside the stove so the dough would rise faster. As she set the timer, she felt pleased with herself. She knew they could do it!

"All done?" Mama asked when she passed the girls on the stairs. Lily and Beth were going upstairs to play in Lily's room.

"Yes, it was easy," Lily said. "Can we make bread every week?"

Mama smiled. "I don't know about every week, but it would be nice if you could do it every once in a while."

It wasn't long before Lily and Beth heard the timer ring. The girls ran downstairs and washed their hands. It was time to punch the bread dough down again. Lily lifted the towel off the bowl and looked at the bread dough. It still looked exactly the same as when she had covered it. She was puzzled.

"Why didn't the bread dough rise?" Beth asked. "We did everything right."

Mama crossed the kitchen and peered over the girls' shoulders. "Did you remember to put the yeast in?"

Yeast? Beth and Lily looked at each other, mouths opened to a big O. They had forgotten all about adding yeast. The bread dough was ruined.

"Go throw it over the fence," Mama said, not unkindly.

Lily scooped the big ball of dough out of the bowl. Beth held the door open for her, and the girls went outside.

Joseph and Dannie ran over to see what the girls were up to. "Another one of Lily's kitchen DIS-AS-TAHs!" Joseph yelped, howling with laughter. Naturally, Dannie laughed, too.

"Whatcha gonna do with it?" Joseph said.

Lily scowled at him.

"Your mama told us to pitch it over the fence," Beth said. She was more patient with the boys than Lily, but then, she didn't have any little brothers.

"Pitch it to me first," Joseph said.

Lily tossed the dough to him. Joseph caught it and pitched it back to Dannie. He tossed it to Beth who tossed it to Lily. She liked how the dough felt—like a big, soft rubber ball. She caught it and pitched it back to Joseph. Finally she had a cooking mistake that was fun!

"Girls!" Mama called from the kitchen door. "Come in and help me start supper."

Lily pitched the dough over the fence. Dozer sniffed at the dough and took a bite. Lily wished she would have had time to see how he liked her yeastless dough, but Mama needed her. Both her and Beth.

Lily loved having Beth stay with her. Everything was double the fun, even the kitchen DIS-AS-TAHs. It was just the way Lily imagined having a sister would be. Beth was Lily's almost-sister.

❦

On Saturday, the whole church had plans to gather at the Rabers' and rebuild their house. On Friday evening, Lily and Beth helped Mama do all the usual Saturday cleaning so they would be ready to leave first thing in the morning.

Right after breakfast, the Lapp family plus Beth piled into the buggy. Dannie sat on the front seat, squeezed between Papa and Mama and Paul, so that Beth could fit in the back with Joseph and Lily.

As Jim clip-clopped down the road, Lily asked Papa why a house took so long to build. "It took a little less than a week to build the schoolhouse," she said. "Most of a barn can be built in a day."

"Houses are a little different," Papa said. "They're much bigger than a schoolhouse and not nearly as simple as a barn. It takes time to do everything right. Once it's completed, though, Beth will have a very nice new home."

As Papa turned Jim into the Rabers' driveway, Lily saw all kinds of people scurrying around the property like bees around a hive. The house looked like a skeleton made up of two-by-fours and a roof. It needed walls and windows and doors to become a home. And love.

Papa strapped his tool belt around his waist and disappeared into a cluster of men. The air was filled with the sounds of hammers hitting nails and men shouting orders to each other. The women gathered in the buggy shed to prepare lunch on little kerosene stoves. Along one wall of the shed were pieces of furniture and stacks of boxes.

"What's in the boxes?" Lily asked. They looked so interesting.

"They're filled with things people gave us to replace what we lost in the fire," Beth said.

Wouldn't it be fun to snoop through all those boxes? Lily would like to see what people donated to Beth's family, but she knew better than to suggest such a thing. Plus, Ida Kauffman was standing nearby.

All day long, people worked hard. By the time the sun

started to set, the walls were up and windows and doors filled the gaping holes. But Lily could see that there was still a lot of work to be done before it became a home.

❦

Later that evening, Lily woke to the sound of voices downstairs. She went down to get a drink of water. Papa and Mama were still up, sitting at the kitchen table and talking. When they saw her, their conversation stopped abruptly, which made Lily all the more curious. What had they been talking about? She went right to the cupboard and reached for a glass.

"Lily," Papa said, "everyone is helping the Rabers since they lost nearly everything they had."

Lily nodded. It was nice that people were helping Beth's family. She filled up the glass with water and took a sip.

"So Mama and I thought it would be nice if you chose something special to give to Beth."

Mid-gulp, Lily started to sputter and cough. She thought it was wonderful that everyone was helping Beth, but she didn't want to give up one of her own special things. If she had to, she could buy something new to give to Beth. Something new would be easier to give than something she loved. Lily put the glass of water down. "Beth liked Pete best."

"Who was Pete?" Mama asked.

"Pete was Beth's pet parakeet," Lily said. "I could buy her a new parakeet." She hoped Papa might offer to give her the money to buy it because she had very little money. Zero, in fact.

"We'll give that some thought," Papa said. "But for now I want you to go back to bed. Think long and hard about something you already have that you can give to Beth."

Lily trudged upstairs. Beth was sound asleep as Lily climbed into the nest bed she had made on the floor. She lay there for a long time, trying to think of something she wouldn't mind parting with. The problem was that she loved everything she had.

It dawned on Lily that Beth had loved her own things just as much.

Lily changed her mind. She would give Beth a candy bowl. No, no. She would do better than that. She would give Beth her very favorite candy bowl. It was a small way of letting Beth know she cared.

⁂

The next Saturday, the Rabers' new house was finished and ready to be moved into. Lily was nearly as excited as Beth. Papa dropped the family off and drove away on a mysterious errand. When he returned, Jim was pulling the spring wagon instead of the buggy. Lily ran over to see what could be in the back of the spring wagon. Papa had built a table and chair set! Jonas Raber thanked Papa over and over. Papa seemed embarrassed. Pleased, though. Jonas helped him carry the table into the kitchen.

Beth and Lily ran through the house to explore every room. They both liked it much better than Beth's old house. When the girls went into Beth's room, Lily gasped. Beth's room had been painted a light pink. Soft white curtains hung at the windows. It looked so beautiful that Lily felt a little ping of jealousy. She tried to squish it down, right away, but it was very hard not to feel jealous. It was a wonderful bedroom for an eleven-year-old girl.

The first thing Beth did was to put Lily's candy bowl on

153

top of her dresser. "There, now it seems perfect," Beth said. Lily thought that was a very kind thing to say. She thought it looked perfect even without a candy bowl.

All afternoon, people bustled around the farm, carrying in furniture and boxes that had been stored in the buggy shed and the barn loft. By evening, the house looked like a real home. People were starting to leave as Mr. Tanner drove up in his station wagon. Papa went over to talk to him and then came back to the house holding a pretty pink bird cage. Inside was a beautiful green parakeet.

Papa handed the pink bird cage to Beth. "Lily wanted you to have another bird," he said. "He can't take the place of Pete, but we hope this one will be a good pet for you."

Beth's eyes filled with tears. She gave Lily a hug and told her she was the best friend anyone could ever have. Jonas Raber started to thank Papa all over again.

Papa gathered the family together to leave before Jonas could embarrass him again with countless thank-yous. "It's time to go home now," Papa said.

When they reached Whispering Pines, Lily went up to her room to bring down a book to read after supper. It had been fun to have Beth stay with her for the last few weeks and now her room was strangely empty. It was the closest Lily had ever come to having a sister. She wanted a sister now more than ever.

The Trouble
with Harvey Hershberger

*E*ffie Kauffman thought Harvey Hershberger was cute. Not as cute as Aaron Yoder, she told everyone, but still very, very cute. The attention she gave him only puffed up Harvey's big head all the more, if it were possible.

Harvey *was* cute, Lily had to admit—though she would never admit it out loud. His hair was bleached by the sun and his blue eyes sparkled. But he was every bit as annoying as he was cute. He never knew when to be funny and when to be quiet.

One of the things Harvey did that irritated Lily was to whistle while the children sang songs in school. It wasn't that Lily minded whistling—Papa was a champion whistler. But Harvey whistled off-key. Teacher Judith never stopped his terrible whistling.

On the afternoons when Mama taught English, before she dismissed everyone, she taught the children new songs. It wasn't long before Harvey's boldness set in. He whistled along instead of singing. The first time, Mama didn't stop him, which was a disappointment to Lily. She thought that Harvey's mother should be sent a note about his off-key whistling. Maybe the new bishop, too.

The second time Harvey started to whistle instead of sing, Mama did something odd. She reached into her desk and pulled out a lemon and a knife. Right in front of everyone, while the students kept singing, Mama sliced the lemon in half and squeezed the juice into a teacup. Mama was up

to something, but what? She took a sip of the lemon juice, watching Harvey the entire time.

Harvey's whistle sputtered to a stop.

On Thursday, Mama had the children finish the day by practicing a new song, just like they did on Tuesday. Harvey started up his horrible whistling. Mama quietly pulled out another lemon from her desk drawer and cut it in half, then squeezed the juice into a cup. She lifted the cup to her lips.

Out of the corner of her eye, Lily watched Harvey. He got a funny look on his face, like his mouth was puckering up at the very thought of the sour lemon. He kept wiggling his lips like a horse, as if he couldn't get them to do what he wanted them to do.

Mama's sour lemon trick was just the thing to cure Harvey of his off-key whistling.

❦

Dear Cousin Hannah,

Today was the worst day of my entire life. It started when I took too long to wash and dry the breakfast dishes (but there was the cutest little chipmunk outside the kitchen window), and then I had to rush to get ready for school. I threw on my coat and completely forgot my cape and apron! I didn't even realize what I'd done until I heard Effie whisper and point and laugh. Of course, that got Harvey and Aaron and Sam laughing at me, too. I wanted to run home during first recess, but I've got near-perfect attendance so far for the year and it wasn't worth jeopardizing my very excellent record. (Teacher Judith says that there will be a special prize for the student who has the best attendance by the end

157

of the term, and so far I am in the lead to win.) So I ended up just wearing my coat all day long.

By lunchtime, the schoolhouse was warm (Mama calls it moulting season), and I started perspiring and my face turned bright red. Of course, Aaron noticed, and he started calling me LilyBeet. I guess that's an improvement on calling me Wholly Lily, like he used to call me. But not by much.

The day just kept getting worse.

Joseph brought horse chestnuts to school. (You are probably wondering why, but I have no idea.) Harvey insisted they were good to eat. Even Aaron told him he was wrong, but Harvey doesn't listen to common sense. (That doesn't mean I think Aaron has common sense. He doesn't.)

After a heated discussion that took up most of lunch recess, Harvey tried to roast the horse chestnuts by putting them inside the furnace. After they were nearly burned to a crisp, he took them out and ate several of them. It wasn't long before he turned green, started to moan, and got sick! His throw-up splattered all over my new shoes. Hannah, it was disgusting. Just disgusting. The room smelled horrible.

The only good thing was that Harvey went home early.

But the day got worse! On the way home from school, I made the mistake of complaining to Joseph that my new shoes were spoiled by Harvey. I might have mentioned that I wasn't terribly disappointed because I wished I'd been able to get shoes with high heels, like I'd seen on an English woman who came into Papa's shop last Saturday. I liked the pecking sound they made on the floor in the workshop.

Well, you know how Joseph likes to make things. He decided to surprise me with a pair of high heels. He pounded a spike through the heels of my brand new, stinky (because of Harvey) shoes. Now they are really, truly ruined.

I should have just stayed in bed.

Your cousin,
Lily

Mama taught English classes to the upper grades on Tuesday and Thursday afternoons. On those days, Lily and Joseph stayed to help Mama clean up the schoolhouse after the rest of the children went home. Mama checked all the English lessons while they waited for Papa to come get them in the buggy.

It was such a beautiful spring day that Lily asked Mama if she could walk home instead of wait for Papa to arrive. Mama looked up from the papers she was grading. "As long as you take Joseph with you, I don't mind if you want to start for home. Leave your lunch boxes and I'll take them in the buggy. If Papa comes soon, we'll pick you up along the way."

Joseph and Lily raced up the road. At the top of the first hill, they stopped abruptly. Just up the road were Becky Hershberger and Ephraim Stoltzfus. They were holding hands!

"Ewww! Look at that," Joseph said.

"Sickening," Lily said. She shuddered at the thought of holding hands with a boy.

A car turned onto the road and Becky and Ephraim dropped their hands. As soon as the car passed out of sight, they locked hands again.

Lily and Joseph walked slowly down the hill behind them. "I don't think they know we can see them," Lily said.

"I don't think so, either," Joseph said. Just then, Becky and Ephraim stopped walking and he leaned his face toward hers. "Ewww! I think they're kissing."

Lily felt like gagging. "Let's run toward them. Stomp your feet as loud as you can!"

Lily and Joseph charged down the hill. Becky and Ephraim startled, looked at them, then ran off down the road. Lily and Joseph slowed down to a walk again, huffing and puffing, pleased with themselves.

During recess the next day, Lily was playing in the outfield during a softball game. Harvey ran out to her. "Your brother Joseph is a liar."

"That is *not* true," Lily said. Actually, sometimes it was true, but Harvey didn't need to know everything.

"He said that Becky and Ephraim were holding hands and kissing on the way home from school yesterday."

"Oh *that*?" Lily said. "I saw them, too."

Harvey was outraged. "I don't believe you, either!"

Lily shrugged. "Suit yourself. But we know what we saw."

The bell rang and Harvey glared at her before he ran to the schoolhouse. Lily wondered why Harvey acted so indignant about Becky's reputation. Lily wasn't at all surprised that Becky was only thirteen and was already kissing boys. Becky was a girl who wanted to be older than her years.

A few days later, Lily and Joseph were walking home from school with Beth and Malinda when Harvey ran up to join them. "I need to talk to you both." He waited until Beth and Malinda turned down a road before he said, "I asked Becky if she and Ephraim were holding hands and kissing on the way home from school, and she said they weren't and that now she knows that Lapps are liars."

Lily gave Joseph a warning look. There was no point in arguing with someone like Harvey.

Of course, silence never stopped Harvey. "I want you both to admit you lied and that you're sorry," Harvey said. "I'm sure she will forgive you."

"But we didn't lie," Joseph said.

"We know what we saw," Lily said. "Your sister is the one who isn't telling the truth."

"Well, Hershbergers aren't allowed to lie," Harvey said.

"Lapps aren't, either," Lily shot back. This was silly. She didn't really care if Ephraim and Becky were kissing. Her only thought about it was that she would definitely never be caught doing anything like that.

"I'm going to prove that you are lying," Harvey said. "I'll give you until tomorrow at one o'clock to confess. If you don't admit you're lying about Becky, God will make your index finger turn black. But if you're telling the truth, it won't change color."

Lily stared at him in disbelief. Was he crazy? He was! "Then we don't have anything to worry about," she said, "because we are not lying! Come on, Joseph. Let's hurry home." She started to run. Anything to get away from crazy Harvey.

The next day at first recess, Harvey came to check Joseph

and Lily's fingers. "If there's a gray tinge, that means they're already turning black. You'll see."

Lily and Joseph held out their hands. Their fingers looked pink and healthy, like they always did.

"Just because I can't see anything yet doesn't mean it won't go black," Harvey said in a voice filled with warning. "Maybe you should just admit you were lying so you won't have to worry all day. Once those fingers go black, they'll stay that way for the rest of your life. Everyone will know that you're liars."

During noon recess, Harvey checked their fingers again and told them they should confess now, before it was too late. Lily and Joseph refused, though they did get a creepy feeling up their spine when he told them. "It *was* Becky and Ephraim, wasn't it?" Joseph whispered.

"Yes! Absolutely!" Lily said, looking at her finger. "I think so, anyway. I'm almost positive it was them. Nearly one hundred percent. Maybe . . . sixty percent positive."

After noon recess, Teacher Judith read a chapter from a book. Lily couldn't concentrate on the story. What if her finger did turn black? She looked over at Joseph. He sat at his desk with his hands spread on the table, staring at his fingers. She had never seen her brother focus so intently on something at school.

Teacher Judith closed the book, put it away, and asked the third grade to come to the front of the classroom for spelling. Lily stared at the clock. Only two more minutes until it would be one o'clock. The second hand never moved so slowly before. *Tick, tock, tick, tock.* Finally, it was one o'clock! Lily squeezed her eyes tight, then opened them to look at her finger. Why, it looked just like it always did! She breathed a sigh of relief, turned to Harvey, and held up her hand with a smug smile. Then she went back to work on her math assignment.

At last recess Harvey checked their fingers one more time. "It's a mystery to me why your fingers didn't turn black," he said, shaking his head. "A pure mystery. Because everybody knows you're lying."

Visiting Teaskoota

As soon as the last of the snow had melted away, Lily and Joseph started to plan for a visit to Teaskoota, the old Shawnee Indian. Mama said they had to wait until the weather warmed up. Finally, on a sunny afternoon in late March, Mama wrapped a chunk of fresh homemade cheese into a piece of cloth and put it into a brown paper bag. "Lily, you and Joseph can take this cheese and an apple pie over to Teaskoota this afternoon."

Teaskoota was almost one hundred years old. He lived off the land in a little log cabin, just like a pioneer. No roads led to his home. Lily and Joseph set off to follow a dim trail in the woods and travel through a long, dark abandoned train tunnel to reach the clearing where Teaskoota lived.

Last summer, after Lily and Joseph had discovered Teaskoota, Papa had gone with them to meet him. Teaskoota liked having visitors. During autumn, on Saturday afternoons, Mama had sent Lily and Joseph to visit with him and bring him gifts from the kitchen. Teaskoota was always happy to see them.

He showed Lily and Joseph how to do all kinds of interesting things, like how he made a wooden yoke for his team of oxen. He taught them the names of different types of plants and how they could be used for medicine or food. Lily liked learning about plants. He showed her how the leaves of mallow plants could be used for tea and the funny little button-like flowers on the mallow plants could be eaten.

Other days, Teaskoota sat on his front porch and showed Joseph how to carve and whittle wood while Lily petted Rufus, his big white dog. Joseph liked to whittle, even though the things he made turned out thick and clumsy. Nothing like Teaskoota's delicate carvings.

But when winter came, Lily and Joseph's visits to Teaskoota came to an end. Lily worried about how he would manage through the winter, but Papa assured her that Teaskoota had survived plenty of winters. He had promised that when spring arrived, they could start visiting him again. And today was that day.

As Lily and Joseph walked along the trail, Joseph said, "When I grow up, I'm going to live just like Teaskoota."

Lily rolled her eyes. Joseph was one for cooking up ridiculous ideas. "You'd get tired of living like a pioneer by the end of a month. By the end of the first week." Lily snapped her fingers. "By the end of the first day!"

"That's not true," Joseph said. "I'd never, ever get tired of it. I would have lots of animals. I could walk around in the woods all day long. I could make everything I need and live in a log cabin. It'd be fun!"

"Well, you can live the way you want to, but I think it would be too lonely and hard to live in the middle of the woods far away from Mama and Papa."

"They could come visit," Joseph said.

Lily decided there was no point in telling him that Mama and Papa wouldn't be visiting him off in the deep woods. Or that he would starve if he had to cook for himself. One thing she had learned about Joseph, if she argued with him, he'd act only more stubborn. He'd probably move out to the barn and try to live like a pioneer right now, just to prove her wrong. Boys just weren't reasonable.

Fortunately, before any more words could be exchanged about living like pioneers, they came to the tunnel. There were still thick icicles hanging down from the ceiling, and they had to walk carefully around big chunks of rock that had fallen down during the winter.

Carefully they made their way through to the other side of the tunnel, and soon they reached the little log cabin. Teaskoota was sitting on the porch, as if he'd been hoping they might just mosey over today from Whispering Pines. He was happy to see them, and even happier to see Mama's treats.

He pulled the cheese out of Mama's bag and took a knife out of the pocket of his dirty overalls. He flicked the knife open, sliced a slab of cheese, and promptly started to eat it—using the knife as a fork. Lily tried not to shudder at the thought of everything else that knife had touched before it was used on Mama's fresh cheese. Disgusting!

After Teaskoota sampled a generous portion of the cheese, he disappeared into the cabin with it, along with Mama's apple pie. "I'm baking sourdough biscuits today," he called to them. His gray head popped out of the cabin door. "Well, come on, then!"

Behind the cabin, Teaskoota had built a fire pit with stones. A small smoldering fire was burning in it. A cast iron tripod stood over the fire. It held a pot that was covered in red embers and ashes. "This is where I do my baking," he said. As he poked at the pieces of burning wood, the fire popped and crackled. Sparks flew into the air and then settled back to gently licking flames. "Seeing as how your mama has sent me plenty of good food, I got to thinking that it might be nice to feed all of you for a change." He straightened up and stretched, one hand on his back. "How would your family like to come over for a meal some fine spring day?"

"Oh, we'd like that just fine," Joseph said quickly.

Teaskoota grinned, pleased. "So when can you come?"

"Papa is busy in his shop during the week," Joseph said. "And on Sunday we'll have to go to church, but the next Sunday we could come over for lunch."

Normally, Lily would silence Joseph with a look for speaking first. He needed constant reminding that he was not the eldest in the family and it was not his place to speak up. But this time, she decided to let him do the talking.

Satisfied, Teaskoota nodded. "I'll see you a week from this Sunday."

Lily wasn't at all sure what Papa and Mama would think about having them accept a dinner invitation to Teaskoota's log cabin without talking to them first. But since Joseph was the one who had done all the talking, he would be the only one to get into trouble.

❧

Two Sundays later, Papa harnessed Jim to the little open buggy. The family was heading out to Teaskoota's home for a meal. Mama hadn't been at all cross with Joseph for accepting Teaskoota's invitation without checking with her first. Lily was happy about that and a little bothered, too. Whenever she had accepted an invitation from Grandma or Beth without permission, she got a talking to. Joseph didn't even get a stern look, which Lily thought was quite unfair. On the other hand, she was excited to go out to Teaskoota's house. It was always an adventure and she was sure today wouldn't disappoint.

Everyone climbed into the little open buggy. Dannie and Paul sat on Papa and Mama's laps. Joseph and Lily stood by the front and held onto the dashboard while Papa guided Jim down the road. Before long they turned off onto a path

that used to be an old railroad trail. Jim walked slowly as
the buggy bumped and swayed. Now and then, Papa would
have to duck his head to keep a branch from hitting him.
Papa was smart to use the open buggy. The top buggy would
never have been able to get through to where they were going.
When they got to the tunnel, Papa called to Jim with a long
"whoa." Everyone climbed out of the buggy and waited by
the tunnel entrance while Papa tied Jim to a tree. They would
walk the rest of the way.

Mama took a few steps into the tunnel, then stopped and
looked at the ceiling and walls, which were dripping with
water. "Daniel, are you sure this is safe?"

"I think it will be fine," Papa said. "This tunnel has been here
for a long, long time. Besides, it's the shortest way to get to Teaskoota's cabin—unless you want to climb over the mountain."

Lily thought it was fun to have the whole family walk
through the dark tunnel together but Mama seemed more and
more uncomfortable. "What a spooky place. I didn't realize
how long and dark the tunnel was. I can't believe how many
times Lily and Joseph have walked through this tunnel."

"We don't mind walking through it," Lily said. "You should
have seen it two weeks ago. Icicles hung from the ceiling all
the way down to the floor."

Mama shuddered. Lily wondered if she shouldn't have
told Mama about the icicles. What if she didn't let them visit
Teaskoota until summer?

Dannie loved the tunnel. He hunted for every muddy water
puddle he could find to stomp in. Lily thought it would be
fun to splash in the mud. If only she were a boy or if only she
were a little younger and didn't mind if her dress got dirty.
But she would be eleven soon and she did mind.

Finally, they came to the end of the tunnel and Mama sighed with relief. When they reached the clearing in front of Teaskoota's log cabin, Mama's eyes went wide. "It looks just like you said it does, Lily. Like a picture right out of a history book."

Like always, Teaskoota sat on a rocking chair at the front of his cabin with his dog, Rufus, at his feet. He rose to meet them and Rufus trotted right behind him. Dannie was all eyes and ears, taking in everything.

"Welcome, welcome," Teaskoota said.

"Something smells good," Papa said, pumping Teaskoota's hand.

Teaskoota couldn't stop grinning. His teeth were missing and his face reminded Lily of a wrinkled apple doll. "I'm making sourdough biscuits and baked potatoes for lunch. It will be ready before too long." He told everyone to follow him to his kitchen—the fire pit behind his cabin.

Mama looked stunned.

"Nothing beats warm sourdough biscuits," Teaskoota said. He carefully raked back ashes and red hot embers to uncover some potatoes. "I think these are ready," he said. Using a rake, he rolled the potatoes out of the ashes and onto the grass.

Lily reached down to pick up a potato. Just as her hand touched it, she heard Teaskoota, Papa, and Mama yell "Don't!" but their warning came too late. She dropped the hot potato, but it had already burned her hand.

Papa and Mama bolted over to examine Lily's hand, which was angry red. It was terribly painful. She tried hard not to cry, seeing as how she would be eleven now and too grown-up to cry, yet she couldn't help but let a tear leak down her cheek. First one tear, then another and another.

Papa ran to get some cold water for her while Teaskoota disappeared into his cabin. He came back outside with a jar of honey and poured some on Lily's hand. Next he put some leaves on it and wrapped it with a long strip of cloth. Lily's hand still hurt, but the honey and the leaves made it feel much better.

"What kind of leaves did you use?" Mama asked.

"Burdock leaves," Teaskoota said. "They help soothe and heal burns." He scraped the ashes off the lid of the cast iron pot. With a metal rod, he lifted the lid off to reveal a pan full of golden brown sourdough biscuits. Despite Lily's injury, her mouth watered at the sight. Teaskoota took them out of the pot and placed them into wooden bowls, then he poured a generous amount of honey over each one.

Teaskoota handed the first bowl to Lily. With her unhurt left hand, she carefully touched the biscuit with her finger to make sure it wasn't too hot before she picked it up. It looked delicious. She took a big bite and started to chew. Then she stopped. The biscuit didn't taste anything liked it looked. It was sour! She managed to choke down the rest. When Teaskoota asked if she would like another, she smiled sweetly and said, "No, thank you." Even Joseph and Dannie and Paul didn't eat more than one bite. Papa and Mama quietly ate everyone's leftover biscuits and burnt potatoes.

After lunch, Teaskoota offered to show the family around his property. He led them down a little path through a patch of trees to a meadow. At the edge of the meadow were several hives of bees. "This is where I get all my honey."

"They look like little box houses," Dannie said. He ran closer to get a better look.

"Dannie!" Papa warned. "Don't get too close."

"Little fella, if you want to see something, let's go look at my chickens and turkeys," Teaskoota said. "I put them in the barn so they didn't disturb our lunch, but I can let them out now." He opened the barn door and the chickens hurried out. The turkeys strutted around in the barn. They looked so silly—as if they were the bosses of the barn.

Dannie chased them and waved his arms. "Shoo turkeys, shoo turkeys! Go out and eat grass." A few turkey hens ran away from him and ducked out the door into the barnyard. The tom turkey stayed put, glaring at Dannie with his beady little eyes. He lowered his head and charged at Dannie, flapping his wings and screeching. Dannie screamed and fell down, then started to cry.

Teaskoota chased the tom turkey out of the barn. Papa helped Dannie get up and brushed the dirt off his clothes. "I think that turkey scared you more than he hurt you," Papa said.

Even as he was wailing, Dannie kept one eye on that tom turkey. "I don't like turkeys," he said.

"They aren't used to little boys," Teaskoota said. "Let's go sit on the porch and visit where no one has to worry about getting hurt."

As Teaskoota and Papa talked about the weather and crops and animals, Lily felt disappointment settle over her. She had been so excited about this visit and everything went wrong. Her tummy was rumbling from hunger because the lunch of sour biscuits and burnt potatoes was terrible, her hand was burned, and Dannie was frightened. And now, all that was left to do was to sit, sit, sit and listen to grown-ups talk. It was no different visiting a Shawnee Indian on a Sunday afternoon than visiting an Amish bishop.

Dozer's Nose for Trouble

Dear Hannah,

I'm sorry it has been so long since I wrote to you. Ever since Mama started to teach English at school, I don't have much time for letter writing. I wish you could have had Mama for your English teacher, too. She makes learning fun and all the children like her.

All except Effie. She keeps telling everyone that Mama is getting fat and should stay at home. Yesterday she said she was sure that soon I will get a baby sister. When I asked her what made her think such a thing, she gave me one of her melting stares, like I was the dumbest thing that ever walked the earth. Then she told me that if I looked very closely at Mama's face, I could see she was hiding an important secret. I don't believe Effie. Long ago, I learned my lesson about Effie's superstitions.

But . . . it would be fun to have a baby sister.

Grandma Miller and Aunt Susie come over on Saturdays to help with the housecleaning since Mama is teaching. It makes the Saturday work go much more quickly.

Speaking of our Aunt Susie . . . here's another story for you. Do you remember that Aunt Susie is afraid of Band-Aids? Harvey and Aaron found out, so they covered their hands with Band-Aids at church and chased her after church was over. They've done it twice now. Last Sunday, I was holding Aunt Susie's hand to help her run away from the boys. It had been raining so we both slipped and fell in the mud. Aunt Susie hurt her wrist and cried. I was so mad at the boys! When Grandma asked what happened, I told her, in a very loud voice. So loud that I hoped those boys' parents would hear. I hoped they would get into big trouble.

But would you believe that Harvey's father, Abe Hershberger, who acts like he's the bishop over everybody, only laughed? No wonder Harvey is insufferable.

> *Your cousin,*
> *Lily*

P.S. The hired boy, Tom, does sound very charming, and I'm glad he's so nice to you and Levi. Just how old is he, anyway?

Early one morning, Papa came in from the barn after doing the chores, smiling from ear to ear. "There's a surprise out in the barn," he said. "Anybody want to go see what it is?"

"We do!" Joseph and Dannie said. Lily was already at the door, getting her coat on. Joseph and Dannie started outside without their coats, but Papa put his hands on their shoulders. "The surprise isn't going anywhere. Let's slow down, get coats on, and walk along with Paul so he can enjoy the surprise, too."

When they reached the barn, Papa slid open the door and waited until everyone was inside. He pointed to Pansy's stall. Curled up in the straw was a beautiful little calf. Pansy was so proud. She licked her calf all over. The calf tried to rise and stand on its wobbly legs. Pansy nudged it with her nose and licked it some more and the calf tumbled down again.

"Is something wrong with the calf?" Dannie said.

"No, it's fine," Papa said. "It just needs a little time to

figure out how to use its legs. I think we should probably leave them alone for now." He held the barn door open and shooed everyone up to the house. Lily couldn't wait to tell Beth and Malinda about the little calf. Effie would act as if calves were born every day at her house, but Beth and Malinda would want to hear all about it.

⁂

Pansy's beautiful calf grew quickly. It liked to bounce around the pen and run in circles around Pansy. She was a good mama and didn't mind. She just kept on chewing her cud, slow and lazy. Lily liked to pet the calf. When she was alone with Pansy and the calf, she called the calf Princess. Her real name was Nelly, which Lily thought was much too ordinary for such a pretty calf. Papa said he wasn't planning to sell Nelly. In a few years, Nelly would be old enough to provide milk. He thought they could use another cow to make all the cheese and butter a growing family needs.

Growing boys, Papa meant. Those little brothers ate twice as much as Lily. They had bottomless pits for tummies.

⁂

Lily was sweeping the front porch when she heard Dozer bark and bark. Then she heard someone yell. She ran down the porch steps and around the corner of the house to see what was causing the commotion. Dozer was barking at Mr. Beal's cows over in the field. Mr. Beal yelled at him to get away, but Dozer paid him no mind. One of Mr. Beal's sons rode up to Dozer in his four-wheeler. He revved the engine and chased Dozer off.

Mr. Beal saw Lily and climbed through the fence. "Is your

176

father at home?" He was an interesting-looking man to Lily: short and bent, and he wore bib overalls with an old wool jacket that seemed almost to reach the ground, even in the summer. He had a blue work shirt buttoned up to the collar, a straw hat with a green see-through visor, and plain glasses so thick his eyes expanded when he looked directly at them. Normally, he was very nice. Right now, he looked mad.

"Yes," Lily said. "He's working in the shop."

Mr. Beal marched through the yard to Papa's shop. He was holding his fist tightly, but Lily couldn't make out what was in his hand. She ran inside. "Mama, Dozer is in trouble again. He was chasing Mr. Beal's cows and now Mr. Beal has come over to talk to Papa."

"That dog!" Mama said. "I have never known a dog with such a nose for making trouble."

Lily agreed. Dozer was nothing but a nuisance.

After Mr. Beal left, Papa came inside to talk to Mama. "Dozer ripped some tags off the ears of some of Mr. Beal's calves. He's not very happy about it. He said he had wanted to sell some of his heifers once they're five hundred pounds but since their ears are torn, their price will drop." Papa took off his hat and turned it in a circle in his hands. "I thought we could give Nelly to him. We'll have to keep Dozer in the shop until he learns to stay at home where he belongs."

NO! Papa was giving away the beautiful Princess calf. It was all that awful dog's fault. Lily was furious with Dozer! She wished someone else had found him on that rock bed last summer.

That afternoon Papa and Joseph led the calf over to the Beals'. Lily sat on the porch steps and watched, still fuming at Dozer. When they returned, Papa sat next to Lily on the porch. "It's much better to give up our calf and keep a good neighbor than to keep our calf and have troubles with our neighbor."

Lily thought it would be better still to give away Dozer and keep the calf.

He was a horrible dog, Dozer was.

Jim

The minute Lily and Joseph turned up the driveway after school, Dannie bolted out of the house with a look on his face like he was about to burst with a secret. "There's a surprise out in the barn!"

"What kind of surprise?" Lily asked. She had learned from experience to be wary of Dannie's surprises. His last surprise involved a mouse in Lily's desk drawer.

"Come look for yourself!" Dannie said and ran to the barn. Lily and Joseph looked at each other and shrugged. They set their lunch boxes on the porch steps and hurried behind Dannie.

Inside the barn was a new horse, standing in a stall next to Jim. This horse was taller than Jim, with a burnt-orange-colored coat. Its ears were pointed forward and the whites of its eyes showed. Lily didn't like this horse, and she was pretty sure he didn't like her. She wondered why Papa would have bothered with a horse like that. She hadn't even known he'd been thinking about getting another horse.

Papa walked up the barn aisle. "Well, what do you think?"

"He's the ugliest horse I've ever seen," Lily said.

Papa nodded. "He may not be pretty, but I hope by the time I'm done training him, he'll be one of the best horses we've ever had."

"What are you going to do with him?" Lily asked.

"I want to train him to be our buggy horse," Papa said.

"But Jim is our buggy horse," Joseph said.

"Jim is getting old." Papa crouched down beside Joseph and Lily. "There are a lot of hills in Cloverdale. It's getting harder and harder for him to pull our buggy up and down all those hills. It's time we had a young, strong horse for all that pulling."

"What's this one's name?" Lily asked. She reached out to stroke the horse's nose, but he jumped back and snorted air through his nostrils. That was one nervous horse. She hoped Papa knew what he was doing.

"He doesn't have a name yet," Papa said. "We'll have to decide on one. But in the meantime, I don't want you to get too close to him. He's not used to children. He's not at all trained. I need time to work with him and gentle him."

Dozer had sneaked into the barn and sniffed near the new horse's stall, which made the horse panic and dance. Papa grabbed Dozer by the collar. "Joseph, you'll need to keep Dozer away from the barn for a while."

"I think we should call that horse Nervous Ned," Lily said.

Papa laughed. "Just give me some time, Lily. I think you'll grow as fond of him as you are of Jim."

Lily knew *that* would never happen. She loved Jim. He had been her buggy horse for as long as she could remember.

When she went into the house, she asked Mama if she knew there was a strange, ugly horse in the barn.

Mama looked up from cutting cabbage for coleslaw and smiled. "Papa has felt that Jim is showing his age. He's been looking for a young horse for a while now and finally found what he was looking for."

"When did we get Jim?" Lily asked.

"Grandpa Lapp gave Jim to Papa a few weeks before we got married," Mama said. "I still remember how happy Papa was to get him. We both thought he was one of the most beautiful horses we had ever seen."

"Jim's such a gentle horse," Lily said. "Not like that Nervous Ned out in the barn."

"He's just young and unbroken." Mama put the chopped cabbage into a big bowl. She sliced off the tops of some bright orange carrots and rinsed them under the sink. "Papa can work wonders with a horse. You watch and see. He won't be nervous for long. Papa will use Jim to help train him."

"I can't imagine petting that horse or letting him eat grass or oats from my hand the way I do with Jim. He was never jumpy like that new horse."

"It did seem as if Jim always wanted to please us. I think he genuinely loves you children." Mama handed Lily a carrot scraper and the carrots.

Lily went to the kitchen sink and peeled the carrots so that Mama could grate them into the cabbage. Carrot peels were splattered all over the sink. Lily handed the peeled carrots to Mama.

"Lily, did I ever tell you about how Jim gave me a scare when you were a baby?"

Lily grinned. She loved being in the kitchen alone with

Mama, hearing her stories. "I don't think I ever heard that story."

"It was in the fall and a killing frost was due in that night," Mama said, grating the carrots with a fast motion. "I was trying to gather the last of the tomatoes in the garden. I had spread a blanket on the grass beside the garden and you were sitting on it as I worked. We still didn't have a real fence for Jim's pasture. Papa had strung wire that Jim probably could have easily jumped out of, but Jim seemed to know he needed to stay inside. He had never tried to jump the fence." She finished grating carrots and handed a big spoon to Lily so she could stir.

Mama went to the refrigerator and came back with a large jar of mayonnaise and a second spoon. She added large spoonfuls of dressing into the coleslaw as Lily mixed it all together. Mixing was Lily's favorite thing.

"On that day, I hadn't been in the garden for more than a few minutes when Jim started acting funny. He pranced nervously and pawed the ground and snorted. He grew more and more agitated. I stopped to see what could be bothering him. He reared up on his hind legs and tossed his head angrily. The next thing I knew, he jumped right over the fence and galloped toward you on the blanket!

"I was so scared. I was sure he was going to crush you. I ran to stop him but I couldn't get there in time. It was terrible! Suddenly, Jim stopped at the edge of the blanket and pawed the ground. He snorted some more, but he didn't step on the blanket. Then I realized what had caused the problem: There was a snake on the ground and Jim had killed it with his hoof. I think he had seen it slither close to you and wanted to protect you. He calmed down right away and I led him back to his pasture."

Lily felt a warm, happy feeling rise from the bottom of her toes all the way to her head. Jim was a fine, fine horse. She would never love another horse. "Did he ever jump over the fence again?" Lily asked.

"No, he never did," Mama said.

"Maybe it's good that Jim can take a rest now and then from the buggy rides, if Papa can ever gentle that ugly horse. But I'll still want my buggy rides with Jim."

Mama opened her mouth, then snapped it shut, as if she was going to say something but thought twice about it. Lily was about to ask her what she was going to say when Joseph and Dannie burst into the kitchen. Their noisy voices woke up baby Paul from his nap and he started to howl. Papa came upstairs from his workshop and soon the kitchen was filled with happy, noisy chaos.

But to Lily, those special times in the kitchen with Mama were always the best.

❦

After considering all kinds of names for the new horse, including many outlandish suggestions from Joseph and Dannie, Papa decided to name him Bob. He worked with Bob every single day. His first goal in training, he told Lily, was to teach Bob not to be afraid of things. Lily and Joseph liked to watch the training sessions. Today, Papa held an umbrella and walked up and down the barn aisle in front of Bob's stall. Bob pawed the ground, watching nervously. Papa put the umbrella down and closed it. He talked to Bob and stroked his neck.

Jim looked over his stall door with mild interest, as if he thought it was all quite amusing.

Papa reached down, picked up the umbrella, and opened it in front of Bob's face. It surprised Bob and he jumped, backing up, trying to get away from it. "Whoa, Bob," Papa said soothingly. He took hold of his halter and coaxed him to step forward again. He talked and petted Bob a little more, and then he closed the umbrella. Bob jumped and tossed his head.

Patiently, Papa kept on opening and closing the umbrella in front of Bob until he learned that it wouldn't hurt him. After a while, instead of jumping back, tossing his head, and pawing at the ground, Bob munched on the hay in his manger, bored as could be. Papa grinned at Lily and Joseph.

Papa went to his shop and brought back a big blue plastic tarp. Then he snapped it open and waved it in the air. Bob was frightened, jumping and snorting, and settled down only as Papa petted him and talked to him in a calm, gentle voice. He had a fine voice, Papa did.

Papa asked Lily and Joseph to hold the edges of the tarp and run through the barn in front of Bob. "Try to flap it as much as you can so it will make noise."

Sure enough, Bob tried to jump away. His ears were pointed back and the whites of his eyes showed his fear. That was when Lily thought Bob was at his most ugliest. Papa kept on talking to him in a quiet voice. It wasn't long before the flapping tarp didn't even faze Bob. "It's important for Bob to be very comfortable with unexpected things when he pulls a buggy. Anything could blow or flap or make loud noises on the road. I want to make him used to all kinds of situations so he will act calm and relaxed on the road, too."

Lily was glad Papa was taking time to train Bob so that he would be a nice, safe horse. She remembered a time when someone's buggy horse had been frightened of an umbrella and had bolted away from the schoolhouse. Mama had to go rescue the girl who was driving the buggy.

A week later, after many training sessions, Papa was able to put a harness on Bob and walk alongside him, holding the reins and teaching him to turn left and right and giddyup and whoa. He even let Dozer run beside them, barking and jumping like he usually did. Bob didn't flinch.

Lily was so proud of Papa. He was doing a fine job with Bob. She still didn't like that horse, but she could see there might be some hope for him.

The next week, Papa decided Bob was ready for something more challenging. "I think Bob understands everything I have tried to teach him so far. Now it's time to take him out on the road."

Papa hitched Jim to the little open buggy and fastened Bob to the side of the buggy shafts. Bob would not be pulling the buggy today. First, he would have to learn what to do on a road by going alongside an older, well-trained horse like Jim.

When Papa returned, he said Bob did very well. "A big dump truck passed us on the road. Its tarp was flapping in the wind, but you would never even have guessed that Bob noticed it. He kept trotting along, just the way Jim did. Bob didn't react to it at all."

Lily was happy to hear that. Soon Bob could pull the buggy by himself and Jim could take a day off now and then.

❧

It was a beautiful April afternoon with a gentle balmy breeze. Lily and Joseph dawdled as they made their way home from school. The ditch beside the road was filled with water from last night's rain. They took turns finding worms and dropping them in the water to see how far they would float.

They jumped up at the familiar sound of a horse and buggy coming around the bend. Lily dried her hands on her apron and picked up her lunch box.

"It's Mama," Joseph said. Jim was trotting toward them with Mama and Dannie in the front seat of the buggy. Baby Paul was in Mama's lap.

Uh-oh. Lily and Joseph had been having so much fun playing that Mama had to come looking for them.

Mama slowed Jim down to a walk. "Whoa," she said as she drew up next to them. "Do you want a ride?"

Lily hopped into the front seat beside Mama while Danny and Joseph climbed into the backseat. "Someone is coming to get Jim tonight," Mama said. "I wanted to drive him one last time, so that's why I came to pick you up."

"Is someone going to borrow Jim?" Lily said.

186

Mama gave Lily a sad look. "They won't be bringing him back. Jim is getting old. We've had him for a long time and he's been a wonderful horse for us, but now it's time to let him relax and enjoy the rest of his life without having to work."

Jim was leaving them for good? Tears sprang into Lily's eyes.

Joseph leaned over the buggy seat. "We could let him relax in our barn."

"I wish we could," Mama said. "I truly do. But it's too crowded in the barn with two horses. It worked while Papa was training Bob, but now Bob is ready to pull the buggy for us. Horses like nice roomy stalls where they can move around. The stall is too small for Jim to stay in if he's not pulling the buggy each day."

Lily felt a heavy sadness cover her heart. The lovely spring afternoon was gone. This was their last buggy ride with Jim. She tried not to cry but first one tear, then another, slipped down her cheeks. She heard sniffing from Joseph and Dannie in the backseat. Even Mama was biting her lip, as if she was trying not to cry. They rode the rest of the way home in silence.

Papa came out of the shop when Mama drove up to the barn. He started to unhitch Jim from the buggy. Mama got out of the buggy and walked up to Jim and stood there stroking his face. Lily was surprised to see tears streaming down Mama's cheeks. Lily couldn't stop her own tears from coming. She cried as she stroked Jim's velvety nose and told him what a good horse he had been. "I'll miss you every day," she said. "You'll always be my special horse." She gave him one last pat and followed Mama into the house.

Mama got a bowl and filled it with potatoes. She set them

into the sink and let cold water run over them before she started to peel them. "It's sad to say goodbye to an animal that was like a member of the family," was all she said. Mama finished cutting up the potatoes and put them on the stove to boil.

Lily started to set the table with silverware. "Mama, do you remember the day Jim backed the buggy into a ditch and the buggy dumped over?"

Mama turned from the stove. "I'd forgotten about that! Poor Jim. I know he didn't do that on purpose, and he did a good job holding still until Grandpa Miller unhitched him from the buggy."

Papa and the boys came in from the barn, and Mama started to dish food into bowls while Lily filled the water glasses. The evening meal was very quiet.

Before they had finished supper, a truck pulling a trailer drove into the driveway. Papa got up from the table. "Does anyone want to come outside with me and say their last good-byes to Jim before he leaves?"

Joseph and Dannie jumped up from the table to join Papa. Mama gave Paul another bite of potato. She didn't look up at Papa. "I said goodbye to him when I came home today. I don't want to watch him leave."

Papa understood. "What about you, Lily?"

She shook her head. "I'll stay in the house with Mama."

Lily wished she didn't hear the clank of the trailer door as it opened and shut, then the sound of the truck engine as it drove away. Jim was no longer their horse. She had lost her appetite and pushed her plate away. She folded her arms on the table and buried her face to hide her tears.

Mama rubbed her back with circles. "Feeling sad at times

like this is normal, Lily. But it helps to know Jim will be happy in his new home."

"But how can we be sure he will be happy and won't miss us?"

"He might miss us a little," Mama said. "But he can make new horse friends. He will get lots of good care where he is going. Papa made sure of that."

As Papa and the boys came back inside, Lily felt a little better. At least she wasn't dreading that final goodbye anymore. But she would never forget Jim. And she would never like Bob.

When Effie Kauffman heard that Jim had been taken away, she told Lily that when horses got old, they were sent off to a glue factory to be turned into glue. "That's not true!" Lily said. "My papa said Jim was going off to a nice farm to rest."

"Oh Lily," Effie sighed, as if she were the parent and Lily were the child. "He just didn't want you to worry."

That afternoon, Lily went down to the workshop and told Papa what Effie had said. Papa stopped varnishing a table and looked up. "Lily, have Mama or I ever lied to you?"

No. Of course not. Effie, though, lied all the time. Lily felt much better.

Weeks passed. Papa was right: Bob had turned into a good buggy horse after all. He hardly ever pointed his ears back now and rarely showed the whites of his eyes anymore. Lily still didn't like him, but she didn't dislike him quite as much. She didn't think she could ever love a horse like she loved Jim.

One Saturday afternoon, Joseph ran down to meet the mailman. Lily used to try to race him to the mailbox, but he was faster than her now and it wasn't fun anymore. Lily watched him from the kitchen window and heard him yell a big "Yahoo!" He ran back to the house waving a big white envelope. "We got a letter from Jim!"

"Don't be silly," Lily said. "Horses can't write."

"Well, Jim probably can, because it's from him." Joseph pointed to the return address: *From Jim.* "You don't know everything, Lily."

"I know more than you and I know that horses can't write."

Mama came over to see what the fuss was about so Joseph handed the envelope to her. She smiled when she saw the return address. "I guess we'll have to open it to see what this is about." She pulled out a pin from her apron belt and slit the envelope open. She drew out several photographs and looked at them before handing them to Lily and Joseph so they could see them.

They were all of Jim. In one picture he was running in a nice green pasture with a white board fence and a long red barn in the distance. In another one, he was eating hay in a big roomy stall in the barn. The next one showed him standing next to some other horses. It reminded Lily of how the men gathered before church, talking about the weather and crops.

Something lifted inside of Lily. She felt so much better now that she knew that Jim was happy. It was very kind of the new owner to send pictures of Jim. Whenever she missed Jim, she could always go look at his pictures again and realize he was happy in his new home.

And she couldn't *wait* to show those pictures to Effie Kauffman.

Aaron Yoder Up to Bat

Spring meant softball games. It was Lily's least favorite game to play during recess. Today was the first day it hadn't rained in a while and the boys were eager to get the game started. Aaron Yoder and Harvey Hershberger chose the teams. Lily was the first player Harvey chose for his team, which even struck Lily as very strange. Usually, she was chosen last because she was a terrible batter. A terrible catcher of balls, too.

Each time Lily was up at bat, she struck out. She tried so hard to hit the ball, but her bat never met anything but air. Harvey didn't seem to mind at all. He was surprisingly encouraging and told her she made a great effort.

The next day, the softball game continued on during recess. Joseph was up to bat when a buggy came clattering into the school yard. They always had to stop the game when a horse was in the school yard and find something less risky to play. They didn't want a foul ball to hit a horse.

Harvey's father, Abe Hershberger, eased out of the buggy and marched up to Teacher Judith. "What's the idea of having the children pick teams to play softball? Don't you know how that starts a competitive streak in children?"

Teacher Judith looked bewildered. Abe Hershberger kept on scolding her until she finally held up a hand to stop him. She whispered something to him and they walked into the schoolhouse to finish the conversation. All the children gathered around the steps of the schoolhouse, trying to figure out what was going on. Abe marched back outside, untied his horse from the hitching rack, jumped into his buggy, and drove out of the school yard without a smile or a wave to his children. Teacher Judith rang the bell early and everyone hurried inside.

The next morning at recess, Harvey said, "I'm not going to play softball today. Dad said no one else is allowed to play, either. He said he would whip anyone who didn't obey that rule."

Aaron Yoder was not so easily fobbed off. "So that's where you get your particular brand of craziness, Harvey," Aaron said, speaking with the authority of one who managed the school yard—and in a way, he did. "No way. We've always played softball and we always will, as long as I go to this school. It's my favorite game." He picked up a bat and ball and walked out on the playground.

Effie Kauffman ran after him. "Aaron, you and I can be team captains, if Harvey doesn't want to play."

"No one is supposed to play softball," Harvey said. Then a light went on in his eyes. "But we can still play ball if we only have one team. The four youngest can be batters and everyone else gets a number. Whoever is number one will be on first base. Number two will be on second. Number three will be on third. Everyone else can be outfielders. When a batter makes an out, he goes to the outfield and everyone moves up one position."

Aaron Yoder rolled his eyes but agreed to the new rules. "If that's how we're going to play, I'll end up being a batter for the rest of this school year. No one will ever get me out."

Aaron's arrogance was insufferable, but Lily knew he was probably right. Aaron would be batting every inning and she would be stuck in the outfield for the rest of the school term.

⚜

Recesses were extra fun on the days when Mama was teaching English. Mama liked to come out and pitch the softball to the batters.

This afternoon, Aaron was up at bat. He hit the ball far to the outfield. Then it was Beth's turn. She swung and missed. Once, then twice. On the third try, she hit a fly ball right to Sam Stoltzfus, who easily caught it and Beth was out. The children all rotated a position and Harvey stepped up to bat. Everybody scattered to the outfield. Harvey always hit the ball hard.

Mama pitched the ball to Harvey. Lily heard a loud crack as Harvey's bat met the ball. It flew right at Mama and knocked her down! Aaron bolted to the pitcher's mound to help her up. Harvey dropped his bat and ran to join them. Aaron and Harvey held Mama's arms and helped her into the schoolhouse.

Lily froze. She wanted to run to Mama but her legs didn't budge. She felt as if her feet were glued to the ground. Beth,

Malinda, and Effie hurried over to Lily. "I hope that ball didn't hurt the you-know-what," Effie said.

Lily looked at Effie, confused. "What are you talking about?"

Beth tugged on Lily's sleeve. "Don't you think we should go see if your Mama is okay?"

The girls ran to the schoolhouse. Inside, Mama sat at the teacher's desk. Her face looked as white as a ghost. Aaron gave her a cloth he had rinsed in cold water. Harvey filled a glass of water for her. Lily quickly ran to Mama's side. "Are you all right?"

"I'm sure I'll be fine in a few minutes," Mama said, but she didn't sound fine or look fine. Everybody swarmed inside the schoolhouse to surround Mama's desk. There was a big lump on her forehead where the ball had hit her. She pressed the wet cloth against her head and closed her eyes. "Really. I'm fine. You can all go out to play."

Aaron gave Mama a concerned look, then he shooed everyone outside. Lily stayed inside with Mama just in case she needed anything. To her surprise, she soon heard the clip-clop of a horse and buggy approach. Papa had come! Lily ran to the window and saw Aaron and Harvey climb out of the buggy with Papa. In the backseat were Dannie and Paul. Harvey and Aaron must have run to Whispering Pines to tell Papa that Mama was hurt.

Papa hurried into the schoolroom. "Rachel, are you all right?"

"I'm fine, Daniel," Mama said, holding the cold cloth to her forehead. "Just a little bump."

Papa gently moved the cold cloth away from Mama's forehead. His dark eyebrows shot up. The lump was even bigger now, as big as a goose egg, turning blue and purple. "I need to take you home. Is there any student who could take your place until school is dismissed?"

Mama's eyes scanned over the eighth graders: Becky, Ephraim, Wall-eyed Walter. "We'd better just let the children go home early."

Papa sent everyone home, then helped Mama into the buggy. He insisted she lie down to rest as soon as they reached home. Tonight, Papa said he and Lily would get supper ready while Mama rested. The next day, she woke up feeling better.

At school the next morning, Effie ran up to Lily. "Is your mama all right?"

"She's doing fine," Lily said, surprised that Effie would ask about Mama.

"When a woman gets hurt during her you-know-what, it means she's in for twice the trouble. It's a fact."

Lily looked at Effie as if she was speaking Chinese. "What are you talking about?"

Effie simply pursed her lips as if the why of it was too obvious to say.

<hr />

Aaron Yoder was up to bat. So far, just like he had predicted, he had never been out. Every day, Lily hoped he would get out. She wanted Aaron to be taken down a peg. Or two. She was banished to the outfield where she would do the least damage to the game, Aaron told her.

Aaron's bat hit the ball with a loud, satisfying crack. Lily watched the ball fly up, up, up before it started to come down. She held out her apron and was thrilled when the ball landed magically in her outstretched apron. All the children cheered!

Someone had finally gotten Aaron Yoder out. That someone was Lily!

Aaron scowled as he headed to the outfield and everyone else moved forward a position.

At long last, Lily was rotating to the infield. She had moved up to third base. Only three more batters needed to get out, then she could have a turn at bat. Now Malinda was up to bat. Despite the fact that Malinda was a very timid, always worried girl, she was a surprisingly strong athlete. She hit that ball far into center field and made it safely all the way to third base. "You did a good job of catching Aaron's fly ball," she said, puffing and panting as she stood on the base. "I wish I had thought to use my apron to try to catch balls."

Sam Stoltzfus hit a ground ball and Malinda ran on to home plate. Junior Hershberger dashed past Lily to Aaron in the outfield. Aaron whispered something furiously into his ear and Junior took off. That was just like Junior. He acted as if Aaron was some kind of hero.

Now Harvey was up to bat. Lily hoped she might catch his ball, too. Maybe today was her lucky day. The ball went up, up, up, right toward her! She opened up her apron and backed up to try to catch it. Back, back, back, then . . . she tripped and landed into something soft and squishy and moist. A steaming fresh pile of horse manure! She jumped up and swatted the back of her dress, trying to brush it all off. Aaron and Junior had dropped to their knees, slapping the ground as they roared with laughter. Junior had sneaked that manure pile out there!

Just when Lily thought Aaron might be getting a tiny bit nicer, he did something rotten! What a *coward*—to get a little boy to do his dirty work. He was an incurable pain. But she was going to concoct a scheme to cure him.

Dear Cousin Hannah,

Thank you for your newsy letter! I'm glad you are enjoying school so much. Since you asked, yes, I do think that Tom the hired boy is too old for you. Ten years is a big difference, especially when you are eleven and he is twenty-one.

I have gobs to tell you. Something funny happened during the softball game at lunch recess today. Harvey Hershberger's little brother, Junior, was catching balls in the outfield and he used his baggy trousers to catch a ball! He's always wearing trousers that are too big for him—probably Harvey's hand-me-downs. He looked so silly! The boys just howled and now they call him Bag Boy. Junior loves the attention—any attention—just like Harvey does.

Last week, Junior put a pile of fresh horse manure behind me on third base, so that I tripped and fell into it. It was all Aaron Yoder's doing. So I thought of a perfect way to get back at Aaron. I filled a pail full of dried horse manure and slipped into the schoolhouse early one morning, silent as snow. Teacher Judith was outside, talking to Effie, as usual, so the timing could not have been any better. I dumped the entire pail in Aaron Yoder's desk! Then I hid the pail in the basement. No one would ever be able to trace it to me.

I could hardly wait to see what Aaron would do. Oh Hannah, I could hardly sit still. Finally, Aaron would be humiliated.

Well, you won't believe what happened. When Teacher Judith asked the sixth grade to get their spelling work-

books out, Aaron opened his desk, shuffled the manure around to find his workbook, took the book out, and closed the lid of his desk. As if a desk filled with manure was nothing unusual to him! When he was up front for spelling, he asked Teacher Judith if he could open the windows, being as how it was a warm day. Of course, she said yes, even though it was a chilly morning. She never says no to anyone.

So Aaron opened up the window next to his desk. All day long, whenever he needed something from his desk, he pitched a few pieces of manure out the window.

Infuriating! Nothing ever bothers Aaron . . . but that never stops him from trying to bother me! I wish he would tease Effie half as much as he teases me. She would love his attention. I loathe it.

Your cousin,
Lily

❦

Only a few weeks of school remained in this year's term. One Monday, right before lunch recess, Teacher Judith told the children to line up, in alternating grades, on each side of the room. "We're going to have a spelling bee. On Friday, the one student still standing will win a special prize."

At the mention of the word *prize*, an epidemic of grins swept through the schoolhouse. Most of them, particularly the boys, would rather work for a prize than eat for a week.

For Lily, this news was straight from heaven. She loved spelling bees and was sure she could win. Wouldn't it be wonderful to win two prizes this year? One for nearly perfect attendance, and one for a spelling bee. Papa would be so pleased.

No sooner had everyone else lined up along two sides of the room than Teacher Judith paired the three eighth graders with the first graders: Wall-Eyed Walter with one of the Hershberger twins, Becky with the other, and Ephraim Stoltzfus with Menno King, who whistled through his missing front teeth when he talked. She paired second graders with seventh, third graders with sixth, and so on. Aaron was paired with Bag Boy Hershberger. Lily was paired with Lavina, her favorite of the little girls. Each time Teacher Judith gave out a word, there was a frenzied conference of whispers. The youngest of the pair would recite the letters aloud. Effie and Toby were the first to drop on the word *affect*. As Effie was waved out of the round, she flounced to her chair and blamed Toby. Pair by pair went down in defeat, until Teacher Judith stopped the bee, to be continued tomorrow.

Rounds of the spelling bee continued each day. By Wednesday, only Lily and Lavina, and Aaron and Bag Boy were left. They spelled down word after word—the entire schoolhouse on the edge of their seats waiting breathlessly for one of the pairs to make a mistake. The room was filled with claps and groans and hoots.

On Thursday, it was a stalemate. "Only one student can win," Teacher Judith said. "So we're going to split up the pairs."

Without Aaron's tutelage, Bag Boy went down in the first round on the word *ransack*. Then Lavina waffled and forgot the *c*. The last two standing were Aaron and Lily. "To be continued tomorrow," Teacher Judith said and announced it was lunchtime.

Lily was determined to take Aaron Yoder down in defeat. She stayed up late into the night, studying words.

꙳

As the clock ticked toward the noon hour on Friday, the entire schoolhouse had a severe case of the fidgets. No one could concentrate with a matter of such import as the spelling bee on their minds. Lily certainly couldn't. Possible words flipped through her mind: *Mississippi*, *preposterous*, *extravaganza*.

By eleven o'clock, Teacher Judith gave up on teaching math to the sixth graders. "Let's go ahead and finish up this spelling bee."

Aaron and Lily bolted to opposite sides of the schoolhouse. They glared at each other from across the sea of desks.

"I'm going to make it a little more difficult," Teacher Judith said. "I'm going to give the definition and let you figure out the word."

Oh, boy. This might be a little harder than Lily had expected it to be. She felt her cheeks flush. Aaron, naturally, looked as if he were enjoying a Sunday picnic.

"Lily, you go first," Teacher Judith said. The entire schoolhouse leaned forward in its chairs. "It contains your vocal chords."

Lily licked her lips. Her mind had gone blank. What was that word? She coughed nervously and suddenly remembered! "Larynx. L-a-r-y-n-x."

"Correct. Aaron, self-confidence or assurance, especially when in a demanding situation."

Oh, Lily knew this one! In her mind she spelled it: a-p-l-u-m . . .

"Aplomb," Aaron said. "A-p-l-o-m-b."

200

"Correct!"

Oh, boy. Lily felt a little bead of sweat on her forehead.

"Lily, your turn. Punishment in return for an injury or wrongdoing."

Lily smiled. This would be easy. "Vengeance. V-e-n-g-e-n-c-e."

As Aaron smirked, Lily realized she had forgotten the *a.*

"Aaron, you try," Teacher Judith said.

"Vengeance. V-e-n-g-e-a-n-c-e."

"Correct!"

The boys in the schoolhouse erupted in hoots and howls. Lily's face felt red enough to ignite. She had lost. She had lost for all the girls. She had lost for herself. She had lost to Aaron Yoder. He had won by spelling *aplomb*—the very thing she accused him of being overly blessed with. She had lost by misspelling the word *vengeance*—the very thing that was driving her to beat him. Shame rippled through her. She deserved to lose. Head hung low, she went back to her desk.

Teacher Judith called Aaron up to her desk and handed him the prize: a box of chocolates. Lily's very favorite kind. If she could feel any worse, she just did.

<hr/>

Lily stayed inside during lunch recess. She didn't want to play softball and be anywhere near the boys. They couldn't stop gloating about Aaron's win.

She put her lunch box back on the shelf and went to the bathroom, then came back inside to read her book. When she opened her desk lid to get her book, she found the box of chocolates that Aaron had won. Was someone playing a trick on her? She hadn't forgotten how sneaky Effie Kauffman had been last year—switching food from children's lunch boxes so that it looked as if Lily was stealing food. "I think there's been a mistake," Lily said. She gave the box of chocolates to Teacher Judith.

Teacher Judith smiled. "Aaron slipped in while you were in the bathroom. He said you deserved the chocolates just as much as he did." She handed the box back to Lily. "I don't think he wanted you to know that he put them in your desk."

Lily was flabbergasted. F-l-a-b-b-e-r-g-a-s-t-e-d. Aaron Yoder might just have a heart, after all.

Mama's Birthday Dress

Mama's birthday was coming soon. Lily tried to think of something special she could make for her. She had already made up her mind that she would not try to bake and decorate a cake. Last year it had turned into a disaster. A "dis-as-tah," as Joseph called her kitchen mistakes.

Lily went into the sewing room to dig through a pile of fabric scraps, searching for inspiration. She dumped several boxes filled with scraps on the floor and sat beside the pile to sort through all of it. Piece by piece, she put the scraps back into the boxes. She put the last scrap into the box and closed it with a sigh. Nothing! She wasn't at all inspired. Maybe . . . she would be inspired if she could use fabric from the piles in Mama's fabric cupboard.

It wouldn't hurt to look at the fabric. She opened the door and admired the variety of colors. They looked so pretty. A purple fabric caught her eye. She hoped Mama would use it to make a dress for her, maybe for a new school dress or a Christmas gift. She ran a finger along the fabric. It felt soft and nice. She wondered why Mama never wore a purple dress. She had different shades of blue, teal, and green, but never purple. Suddenly Lily felt selfish. Mama always saved the prettiest fabric to make dresses for Lily. She tried to envision Mama wearing a dress made with this pretty purple fabric. It would look beautiful on her, with her thick, wavy dark hair and rosy cheeks. Papa would be sure to whistle, one note up, one down, and say something nice when he saw her wear it.

Inspired! That's how Lily felt. She made up her mind. She would use this fabric to make a dress for Mama's birthday. She had never sewed a dress before, but it didn't look very hard when she watched Mama sew. No problem. She was sure she could do it.

Digging through the pattern basket, Lily found Mama's dress pattern. She listened for the sounds of Mama in the kitchen, then quickly darted up the stairs with the fabric and the patterns to her room and locked the door.

Lily spread the fabric on the floor, placed the pattern on top and started to cut. The thin paper pattern shifted as she cut so she placed a few books on top of them to try to keep them still.

When the last piece had been cut, she folded it all carefully, put it into a grocery bag and tucked it under her bed. She would have to find an excuse to visit Grandma Miller soon and sew the dress. That way, Mama wouldn't see what she was doing and, if she needed help, Grandma would be right there to help her. But . . . Lily was quite sure she would not need help.

A few days later, Mama asked Lily to take a recipe over to

Grandma Miller's house. Lily asked if she could stay there for a while, and when Mama said yes, Lily ran upstairs and grabbed the bag that held the purple fabric pieces that she had cut out for Mama's birthday dress. She ran all the way to Grandma's house. She could hardly wait!

Aunt Susie opened the door and welcomed Lily inside. Her eyes went right to the bag in Lily's arms. "What do you have in the bag?"

"I'm going to sew a dress for Mama's birthday," Lily said. Aunt Susie was disappointed that Lily hadn't come to play dolls or color in books today. When Grandma Miller heard Lily's plans, she smiled. "Of course, we'll help," she said. She opened up her sewing machine and threaded the needle with purple thread.

Lily spread all the pieces out on the table, unsure of what to do next. Maybe . . . she did need a little help. Grandma examined all of the pieces she had cut, picked up two pieces and told Lily to sew the seams together. The treadle on Grandma's sewing machine pumped easily, more easily than Lily's old sewing machine, and it didn't take Lily long. "What's next?"

Grandma Miller held Lily's freshly sewn seam, frowning. She tugged at the seam a little and tried to smooth it with her hands. "Which way did you place the pattern on the fabric to cut it out?" she asked.

Which way? Did it matter? Grandma Miller explained that the fabric had a nap to it, and it was important to cut it with the nap rather than against it. Now, even if Lily took special care to try to sew nice straight seams, they gathered together in a twisted, rippled way. Lily felt her happiness start to slip away.

"There is nothing we can do about it now," Grandma said.

"Hopefully we'll be able to iron it really well to make it look a little better."

"I hope so, too," Lily said, starting to fold and pin pleats in the skirt.

"I hope so, three," Aunt Susie said. "Because it looks awful."

❧

Mama's birthday arrived on a cool day in May. She'd said she didn't want a big birthday celebration this year, so Papa hadn't invited anyone to come for a special birthday dinner. Lily hoped Papa would still give Mama a gift. He always chose special surprises for Mama's birthday. Lily thought it would be sad if she didn't end up with any presents other than the purple dress with the bunched seams. At the very least, she thought, purple always made everything better.

As everyone sat down at the table for supper, Lily handed Mama a box that Grandma had helped her wrap. Mama opened it carefully and drew out the purple dress. She held it up, oohing and aahing over it. "Did you make this by yourself?"

"I cut it out by myself," Lily said, "but I took it over to Grandma so she could tell me how to sew it."

"If you don't mind waiting to start eating," Mama said, "I think I'll go change into this dress right now."

"Go right ahead, Rachel," Papa said, winking at Lily. "We'll wait patiently, won't we, boys?"

Joseph and Dannie looked longingly at the bowl of steaming mashed potatoes.

When Mama came back into the kitchen, Papa let out a long low whistle, one note up, one note down. It was just the way Lily had imagined it! "You look as pretty as a posy," he said. His eyes were smiling as he watched her. Purple was definitely the right color for Mama.

Before Mama sat down, Papa raised a hand. "Since it's gift time, I have something for you too."

Dannie leaned next to Joseph and whispered, "I thought it was supper time."

Papa ignored him and rose from his chair. "Let's all go down to the shop."

Everyone followed Papa down the stairs. Lily wondered what Papa had made for Mama's birthday.

Papa led Mama to the back of the shop where several tables and chairs were waiting to be picked up by the customers who had ordered them. He stopped at a beautiful table with six chairs. "I made this table and those chairs for you," he said.

"Oh, Daniel! Thank you!" Mama reached out and stroked the top of the table. "It feels like satin."

Papa chuckled as he watched Mama examine the chairs. "There's an old saying: Cobblers' children have no shoes. I didn't want anyone to say that a furniture maker's family goes without furniture. It's about time we got rid of our rickety old table and have a nice one."

"I didn't mind using our old table," Mama said.

"I know you didn't," Papa said. "But you deserve nice furniture and this table is the first of more to come."

"Oh, Daniel," Mama said again. Her eyes got that shiny look, as if she might cry.

"If Joseph and Dannie can give me a hand, we can carry this thing up to the kitchen and have our first meal on it tonight. It only seems right that a beautiful birthday girl should get to eat at a nice new table."

Mama blushed with all of Papa's compliments. Lily loved hearing them.

By the time the table and chairs had been moved to the kitchen, the supper was almost cold. But no one minded, not even Joseph and Dannie. Mama had a wonderful birthday. The best ever, she said.

※

Lily liked to wash the new table off after every meal. The beautiful, glossy varnished top was so pretty and shiny. Even Joseph and Dannie helped set the table for every meal without being asked.

A few days after Mama's birthday, Lily walked into the

kitchen to get a drink of water after planting beans in the garden. She stopped in her tracks as she saw Joseph and Dannie scrubbing the table with a stainless steel scouring pad.

"What have you done to Mama's beautiful table?" she gasped.

The boys stopped their scrubbing. Joseph looked a little more closely at the table and his face turned a funny shade of grayish white when he saw that the beautiful glossy varnish had been scratched off.

"What are you doing?" Lily asked again. Even to her ears, her voice sounded screechy.

"We were coloring a picture for Papa with markers," Joseph said. "The markers soaked through the paper and stained the table. We tried to wash them, but they wouldn't wash away. So then we thought of the stainless steel scouring pad because that's what Mama uses when she washes pots that are extra dirty. I didn't know the varnish would come off, too." He looked and sounded miserable. Dannie nodded alongside him, looking a little less miserable.

Lily felt sorry for Joseph. She knew just how he felt. Accidents happened. They happened all the time. "You both need to tell Mama what happened."

Joseph looked as if he was going to be sick. She knew he would rather run and hide than tell Mama he had ruined her birthday table. But slowly, he walked out the door with Dannie following behind. Lily drank her water very, very slowly. She wanted to be inside when Mama saw her beautiful table was no longer beautiful. She felt sorry for Joseph, but not so sorry that she didn't want to see him get into trouble.

Mama did look sad as she saw the table, but she assured Joseph and Dannie that Papa would be able to fix it. "He'll have to sand down the table top to remove the varnish that is on it now, then re-varnish it."

"I can help him sand it," Joseph said.

"Me too," Dannie echoed.

"I'm sure he'd like your help," Mama said. She tousled their hair. "Run along and play now."

Lily was astonished. She wondered how Mama could stay so sweet even with little boys who had ruined her table. She knew how much Mama treasured that table.

Then she thought of all the times Mama had been patient with her when she had made mistakes. She couldn't even think of a time when Mama lost her temper. Lily made up her mind that if she ever had children—and she was sure she never would—but if she did, she hoped she would be just like Mama.

Nearly Losing Dannie

It was almost three o'clock in the afternoon. The students stood at their desks, waiting for Teacher Judith to dismiss them. "Anyone who has a brother or sister starting first grade in the fall," she said, "please tell your parents that Friday will be preschool day."

Lily and Joseph shared a look of excitement. Dannie could come to school for a day! He had turned six on his last birthday and would be ready to start school in the fall. She hoped Teacher Judith would let Dannie sit next to her instead of Joseph.

At home, Lily rushed through the door ahead of Joseph to announce the news. After all, she was the oldest. She was always telling Joseph that she should be the one to make the school announcements. When Dannie heard the news, he was stunned speechless, which was a rare event for him. It hadn't occurred to him that he would be going to school one day.

He ran to find Mama. "Mama, pack my lunch box for me right away! I need to go to school!"

Mama laughed. "I think it might be wise to wait to pack it until Friday morning when I get Lily and Joseph's lunches ready."

Dannie hopped through the house on one leg, chanting a singsongy verse: "I'm going to school next Friday! I'm going to school next Friday!" Over and over and over.

Lily sighed and covered her ears. Friday was four long days from now. She hoped she wouldn't have to listen to Dannie's off-key song until then.

When Friday morning finally arrived, Dannie woke before anyone else, even Papa. So early the chickens hadn't started clucking yet. He was worried that Mama would forget to pack his lunch. Lily was relieved when Mama suggested they should start for school a little earlier than usual. Dannie wasn't used to walking that far and it would probably take longer.

But Dannie didn't mind the mile-long walk to school. In fact, he wanted to run the entire way to get there sooner. Lily and Joseph had to convince him that they would get there in plenty of time by walking.

Teacher Judith had placed a small desk for Dannie next to Lily's desk. There were two other little children visiting today, too. Three little desks. Dannie was disappointed that it was so small, that it wasn't filled with books like Lily's. There was nothing in Dannie's little desk except a pencil and a box of eight crayons. Joseph was disappointed that Dannie wasn't next to him. Lily wasn't at all disappointed.

Teacher Judith handed several pieces of paper to each of the three preschool children. Lily leaned over to whisper directions to Dannie. One was a color-by-number, so Lily colored the number code for Dannie because he couldn't read yet. It wasn't long before Dannie had finished it and nudged Lily with his elbow. "I'm ready for another paper," he whispered. His front teeth were gone, so he whistled and spit when he talked.

Lily read the instructions. Dannie needed to cut out the little pictures at the bottom of the page and glue them in the correct boxes. She handed him her pair of scissors and then tried to concentrate on her own schoolwork. She was hard at work on an arithmetic problem when Dannie asked her for glue. School had started only thirty minutes ago and Lily was already tired of having Dannie sitting next to her, interrupting her. She was starting to wonder if she would be able to get her own work done on time today.

Lily couldn't find any glue in her desk. Teacher Judith kept a basket of school glue on the bookshelf. She looked up at the front of the schoolroom. Teacher Judith was having a class, and Lily didn't want to sit with her hand raised until she was noticed. She had too much work to do. She whispered to Dannie, "Raise your hand. When Teacher Judith asks what you need, ask if you can get some glue." She doubted he would say anything, but it was good for him to learn the rules.

Dannie's hand shot up to the ceiling. In his loudest voice, he announced, "Teacher Judith, I need glue."

Everyone swiveled in their chair to stare at Lily and Dannie. Aaron Yoder and Sam Stoltzfus started to snicker. They knew. Only the big boys ever spoke out in class like that and they weren't supposed to! Lily was mortified. What happened to her shy-as-a-church-mouse little brother? She wished she could slip under her desk and disappear. Teacher Judith smiled at Dannie and said, "Lily, you can go get some glue for your brother."

Lily walked over to the glue basket and brought glue back to Dannie. She glanced at the clock. Six and a half hours to go. She couldn't wait for this day to be over.

Lily trudged way behind Joseph and Dannie on the way home from school that afternoon. She couldn't tolerate one more moment of Dannie's endless questions and interruptions. It made her worry about the next school term, in the fall, when Dannie would be a first grader. She only hoped her desk with the other sixth graders would be far, far away from his. He was nothing but a pest.

⁂

The next morning, Dannie lay on the couch clutching his stomach. "Mama, my tummy hurts so bad," he said.

Mama made a cup of peppermint tea and told him to sip it slowly. Normally, Dannie ate or drank anything. He turned his head away, refusing even a tiny sip.

Mama was worried. It wasn't like Dannie to be still, even if he wasn't feeling well. She covered him with a blanket. "Try to sleep, Dannie," she said. "Maybe when you wake up, you'll feel better."

Lily put her hands on her own tummy to make sure nothing was hurting. Whatever Dannie had, she didn't want to catch it. She was determined to stay healthy so she wouldn't miss a single day of school. She was so close! Just two more weeks to go. She wanted that prize for nearly perfect attendance.

Grandma Miller had told her, "An apple a day keeps the doctor away." Ever since, Lily ate an apple every day. She thought it was definitely helping. Dannie ate plenty of apples, though, more than Lily did. Then she thought of another of Grandma Miller's saying—something about eating too many green apples could make a person sick. Maybe that's why Dannie had a bellyache. Too many green apples. It sounded like something Dannie would do.

Every few minutes, Mama checked on Dannie again. He was moaning and groaning. She put her hand on his forehead to see if he had a fever. Finally, she went down to the shop to get Papa. When he came upstairs, he kneeled down next to Dannie. He brushed the hair off Dannie's forehead. "How are you feeling?" he asked.

"Oh, Papa, it hurts so bad," Dannie said. It sounded like a squeak.

"Just lay here as quietly as you can," Papa said. "I'll go call a driver to take us to the doctor."

Papa ran over to Mr. Beal's house to call Mr. Tanner to take them to the doctor. Mama turned to Lily. "Lily and Joseph, I want you to take Paul over to Grandpa and Grandma Miller's and stay there until we get back."

Lily helped Paul climb into the red wagon. Lily and Joseph took turns pulling the wagon down the driveway and along the road to Grandpa's house. They were almost there when Mr. Tanner passed them in his big blue station wagon. Lily hoped the doctor would give Dannie some medicine to make him feel better. She hoped they would come home soon. She didn't want to stay at Grandpa and Grandma's for weeks and weeks, like they did when Dannie and Paul had the chicken pox.

Aunt Susie was happy to see them come to the door. She hurried to get her favorite book to read to Paul. Lily liked Aunt Susie's book *A Big Ball of String*. She liked the pictures of the little boy and his ball of string. That little boy had fun with his string even when he had to stay in bed. Maybe, Lily thought, if Dannie was really sick, then she and Joseph could go out to the barn and roll up all the twine into a huge ball for him. He could play the same way as the little boy in the book.

Dannie would be fine, she assured herself. *Everything will be fine.* Just yesterday, he had gone to school and made a big pest of himself.

Everything would be fine.

❦

Papa didn't return for Lily and Joseph until later that evening. When Grandpa Miller opened the door, he asked if Dannie was all right. There was a tone of concern in Grandpa's voice that worried Lily.

Papa came into the kitchen and took Paul from Grandma's arms. "Dannie had to have surgery to remove a ruptured appendix," Papa said. "Rachel is staying with him overnight. He's a very sick little boy."

Lily felt sorry for Dannie. She didn't know much about hospitals, but Effie had told her that doctors walked around poking people with needles. Poor Dannie.

"We had a good doctor who recognized all the symptoms and sent him straight to the hospital," Papa said. "The doctor said Dannie will need to stay there for a few days."

"Do you want the children to stay here?" Grandma asked.

"No, I'll take them home with me," Papa said. "They'll get a good night's sleep in their own beds."

On the walk home in the dark, Lily looked up at the stars. How could things have changed so quickly? Yesterday, Dannie was fine. Tonight, he was a sick little boy. She said a prayer for Dannie. She hoped he would come home soon. She wouldn't even mind having him come to school again.

✦

It felt strange not to have Dannie at home. Mama or Papa took turns staying with him each day at the hospital. Lily thought he would just be in the hospital a few days, but then he got an infection and had to stay longer. It was a continual worry to Lily.

In the middle of the week, Lily put the last breakfast dish into the cupboard and wiped the countertop. She grabbed the lunch boxes off the counter and went down the basement steps and out the door to Papa's shop to tell Joseph it was time to leave. He was trying to build a toy tractor and was sorry to have to set it aside for school. Joseph felt there was no reason to go to school on any day, but especially so on days he had a project going on in Papa's shop.

Lily and Joseph had just turned onto the road that led to the school when Aaron Yoder came jogging across the field. Usually, he ran right past Lily, unless he stopped to jump in a puddle to splash her or stick out his tongue at her—though she had to admit, that kind of thing wasn't happening as much as it used to.

On this morning, Aaron caught up with them and walked along beside them. "How's Dannie?"

"He's sicker," Joseph said. "He's got an infection in his incision." He admired Aaron, which was something Lily could not understand.

"He'll be fine," Lily said, not wanting Aaron to know their private family news.

"Those doctors will take good care of him," Aaron said. "He'll be home before you know it. Just wait and see."

"I hope he's home before school gets out," Joseph said. "I have a lot of plans to go visit Teaskoota this summer. Dannie's old enough to go with us."

Aaron frowned. "I don't think you should be going through that train tunnel for a while."

"Why not?" Lily asked.

"Last week, I saw a mother bear and her cubs walk into it."

Black bears were a common sight in the woods of Pennsylvania. Joseph shrugged. "Teaskoota's dog would chase them off." He kicked a rock down the road. "I can't wait until the end of the school term. I had to quit making a toy tractor in the shop this morning just to go to school. School is a complete waste of time. I'll never need to know which president was the shortest or which state produces the most corn."

Aaron glanced at Lily over Joseph's head. "Maybe we don't need to know those facts, but I think knowing that kind of stuff is sort of interesting. Don't you, Lily?"

"I like to learn about most things," Lily said. Not math, but most other things.

"Me, too," Aaron said.

Joseph stopped to bend down and tie his shoelace. Lily kept on walking and so did Aaron. When Joseph caught up with them, Lily was irked that Aaron didn't move over to let her brother walk in the middle between them.

The next day, Aaron again caught up with Lily and Joseph to walk to school, and he walked right next to Lily. It was so irritating! Aaron might not be quite as mean as he used to be, but there was no reason he needed to act so chummy with her. They were *not* friends. Why couldn't Aaron just leave her alone and ignore her? That's what she did to him. He was invisible to her. She decided it was time to have a talk with Joseph.

The next morning, Friday, Lily caught sight of Aaron as he emerged out of the woods and started to jog over the field to catch up with them. "Joseph," she whispered. "I don't like it when Aaron walks beside me. Stay by my side so it doesn't happen."

"Okay," Joseph said.

When Aaron caught up with them, he slipped in right between them like he had been doing all week. "Aaron," Joseph said, "Lily doesn't like it when you walk beside her."

Aaron sprang to the other side of Joseph. Lily was mortified. How embarrassing! How could Joseph be so blunt?

Later that afternoon, as soon as they were close to home and no one could overhear her, Lily scolded Joseph. "You weren't supposed to say that I didn't want Aaron to walk beside me!"

Joseph looked confused. "But that's what you said."

"But you weren't supposed to say so! If he tries to walk beside me on Monday, don't say anything about it. I would rather walk beside him than be embarrassed like that."

"Okay," Joseph said, looking hopelessly confused. "But I only said what you told me."

On Monday, Aaron caught up with them and made a point to not walk beside Lily. She was relieved. Everything was going to be fine. Then Joseph said, "Hey, Aaron. Lily wants you to walk beside her after all."

Lily was horrified! What was wrong with Joseph?

Aaron didn't budge. He just stayed right beside Joseph. When Joseph stopped to pick up a rock, Aaron whispered to Lily, "Joseph is being a real pest, isn't he?"

Lily looked at him in surprise. Could it be that Aaron

was actually turning into . . . a nice boy? "A huge pest," she said. It felt strange to not feel angry with Aaron Yoder about something or other. It was a very new feeling for her.

❧

Dannie stayed in the hospital for nine long days. Mama or Papa was with him every day. When the doctor finally said he was ready to go home, Papa and Mama planned a celebration to welcome him home. Papa moved Lily's old twin size bed into the kitchen for Dannie to lie on. Mama set a little stand beside it and placed a picture book and a few of his favorite toy animals and tractor on it.

At the hospital, Papa asked Dannie for a list of store-bought food he'd like to eat, then bought every single thing on the list. Every single thing! Lily thought it might be worth staying at a hospital if it meant she could get any store-bought food she wanted. But then she thought of those doctors, walking around jabbing people with needles, and she changed her mind.

Grandma and Grandpa Miller and Aunt Susie came over to welcome Dannie home. Lily walked from window to window hoping to catch a glimpse of Mr. Tanner's car as it rolled up the driveway with Papa and Mama and Dannie in it. Finally, Grandma said, "Lily, you'll just wear yourself out pacing like that."

Aunt Susie smiled and patted the bag she held on her lap. "You could sit and wait like I'm doing," she said. "I don't want to be too tired to read this book to Dannie when he gets here." She pulled *A Big Ball of String* out of the bag.

Lily hadn't planned anything for Dannie's homecoming. Maybe he would like to play with the busy book she and

Grandma had made when he had the chicken pox. Or maybe he would be hungry for a tomato. Lily's mouth watered at the thought of the big store-bought tomatoes that were waiting for Dannie. They were on his list of food. Lily loved tomatoes. She hoped she could at least get a tiny taste of one. How wonderful to have a tomato before summer started.

"They're here!" Joseph said. He ran to the door and flung it open as Papa carried Dannie up the porch steps and into the house. He placed Dannie gently on the bed they had prepared for him. He didn't look like Dannie. This boy was skinny and pale, with dark blue circles under his eyes. Then he saw Lily and gave her a toothy grin. It was Dannie! He was going to be all right.

Aunt Susie hurried over to his side and smoothed his covers. She held up the book she had brought along. "Do you want me to read to you?"

Dannie nodded. His smile grew even bigger. Aunt Susie climbed next to him on the bed and started to read. She held the book up high so Dannie could see all the pictures.

Lily thought of the tomatoes that waited in the refrigerator in the pantry. "Mama, can I go fix a tomato for Dannie?" she asked.

"Wait until he's hungry," Mama said.

"I'm hungry now," Dannie said.

Now Lily knew that Dannie was definitely going to be fine.

Lily picked out a tomato and sliced it carefully. Probably, Dannie wouldn't mind if she had one tiny slice. She popped a piece into her mouth and practically gagged. This tomato didn't taste anything like the ones that grew in Mama's garden every summer. It had hardly any flavor at all and the texture was odd. Mushy. Ugh. How disappointing.

Friday morning was the last day of school. It would last only a few hours—just enough time for each student to receive his report card and for Teacher Judith to give the usual "I have enjoyed all of you and can't wait until next term" talk. Of course, there would need to be time allowed for the prize to be given out for nearly perfect attendance. Finally, Lily would win something!

Lily waited patiently as each student was called up to Teacher Judith's desk and told he or she would be promoted to the next class. This year, it seemed to take forever. Finally, it was time for the announcement of the prize. Lily sat up straight in her desk. Effie glared at her. She had Effie beat by one day.

"Lily Lapp, you have earned the prize for best attendance." Teacher Judith handed her a heavy gift, wrapped in newspaper.

Lily was so excited! She unwrapped the gift and discovered a beautiful leather-bound book with colored illustrations inside. *Treasure Island* by Robert Louis Stevenson. Even the boys were interested in it. They leaned across the aisles to get a good look at it. It was the most beautiful book Lily had ever been given. She hugged the book close to her.

"And now, class," Teacher Judith said, "I'm sorry to say that I won't be coming back next year. I don't know who your new teacher will be, but I am sure you'll be as wonderful for her as you've been for me."

The class froze. Even Effie wasn't privy to that news. She seemed just as surprised as everyone else. Teacher Judith stood at the door and shook each student's hand to say goodbye. Lily wasn't sure why Teacher Judith wasn't coming back to teach but had a hunch it had something to do with her lack of interest in English lessons.

She wasn't really sure if she would miss Teacher Judith or not. She wasn't a bad teacher, but she wasn't a very good teacher, either. Better than Teacher Katie, not as good as Teacher Rhoda. Lily would be worried, all summer long, about who the next teacher would be.

But she did have a beautiful new book to remember Teacher Judith. She couldn't wait to get home and read it. How wonderful! This was going to be a wonderful summer.

As Lily came into the house, Mama met her at the door and put her finger to her lips. "Dannie is sleeping."

Lily hung her bonnet on the wall peg. She looked at Dannie, sleeping on the bed. He looked so weak and small and pale. Mama said it would take a long time for him to be the same Dannie. Most of the summer, she thought.

Lily tiptoed over to him and tucked *Treasure Island* under his pillow. He needed it more than she did.

⁂

Two Sundays later, Uncle Jacob stood up at the end of church services with an announcement: "Daniel and Rachel Lapp need our help to pay off their recent hospital bill for their son Dannie."

Lily cringed, horrified. This was just the kind of fodder Effie Kauffman enjoyed. Her tongue flapped at both ends. She would use it to remind everyone that the Lapps were too poor to pay their bills. Lily felt so embarrassed for Papa and Mama. She glanced across the room at Papa. He didn't look at all embarrassed.

On the way home from church, Lily asked Papa why Uncle Jacob had to make such an announcement.

"Well, he said it because it's true," Papa said. "The hospital bill was quite costly. Mama and I have always tried to help others when they've been in need. This time, we're on the side of needing help. It's nice to be part of a community where everyone pitches in and helps each other."

Over the next few weeks, Uncle Jacob dropped by Whispering Pines with donations for the medical bills. As expected, Lily and Joseph were shooed off to their rooms whenever Uncle Jacob came to talk, and they took their usual perches at the head of the stairs to listen. It made a dent, Lily heard Papa tell Uncle Jacob, but the bill was still quite sizeable. Papa said he wanted to go to the doctor's office to see if he could set up a payment plan so that he could pay off the bill month by month. "It will still take years," she heard Mama say. Even from the top of the stairs, Lily could sense the worry in her voice.

The next morning, Mr. Tanner arrived to drive Papa to the doctor's office. A few hours later, Papa returned to Whispering Pines. Lily and Mama were hanging clothes on the clothesline as Papa walked over to them, grinning for all he was worth. "Rachel," he said—and Lily could hear the relief in his voice—"the doctor wondered if I would make furniture for his house in exchange for the money we owe him."

Mama clasped her hands together. "Daniel, that's amazing!"

The big grin was still on Papa as they walked to the house. "I thought doctors like him didn't exist anymore, but God's goodness prevailed. He made a way so we can get our bills paid."

It felt like a new morning at Whispering Pines.

Kentucky Auction

*L*ily and her family had been driving in Mr. Tanner's stuffy station wagon for hours. It felt like she'd been in the car for the whole month of July. They were heading to Grandma Lapp's home in Kentucky to help sell Grandpa's things at an estate sale. Lily could hardly wait to see all her Lapp girl cousins again. She had met them at her grandfather's funeral last summer. This would be their last trip to Kentucky because everything was changing.

Uncle Ira and Aunt Tillie were moving to a new community to be closer to their married children. Grandma Lapp would be left all alone and that would never do. Papa and Mama had talked about it and invited Grandma to come live with them in Pennsylvania. Lily was thrilled when she heard that Grandma said yes!

Papa and Mama had moved all the furniture out of the living room and sewing room and into the kitchen. Dannie had improved enough that he could sleep back up in his own bed, so at least the twin bed was gone. The kitchen had seemed enormous until Papa's big desk, a couch, two rocking chairs, and Mama's sewing machine were squeezed into it. Now the room felt small, but cozy and friendly.

By the time the sun was high in the sky, the station wagon arrived at Grandma Lapp's house. Lily was excited to see that her relatives were already there, working and talking and laughing. She was eager to find her cousin Rosie. As she opened the car door, Mama put a hand on her shoulder. "Let's go inside and say hello to Grandma before you go join your cousins."

Grandma was frying some red beets in a pan at her wood cookstove and turned in delight when she heard Papa's voice. Several aunts were busy preparing food for lunch. Lily's eyes scanned all the delicious foods that were being prepared. But her nose wrinkled at the strong smell of the beets. She caught a glimpse of the pastries and cookies and decided she might be able to stomach a few beets if that meant she could have dessert.

As soon as Lily said hello to Grandma, she ran outside to look for Rosie and found her under a tree, sitting with the other girls. Rosie made a spot for her and she sat right down, eager to hear what the girls were talking about.

It wasn't long before Uncle Ira rang the dinner bell. Everyone went to wash up and get ready to eat. There were too many relatives to sit at a table so they gathered in the front yard for silent prayer. The boys were the first to fill their plates with food, followed by the girls. This was one of those moments when Lily wished she were a boy. By the time Lily and the rest of her same-aged girl cousins filled up their plates, some of the bowls of food were already empty. There were still plenty of beets but Lily was delighted to see that her cousins passed them up. She sailed past the beets bowl and hurried to the bowl filled with clouds of mashed potatoes.

All afternoon, everyone pitched in to help get Grandpa's things ready for the auction. Uncle Ira and Aunt Tillie's things, too, since they were moving and giving up farming. Uncle Ira was selling all the animals except the buggy horse, all the farm machinery, and some furniture and things they didn't want to move from the house.

The next morning, Mama helped Grandma Lapp and Aunt Tillie with the food stand. All the other aunts were helping, too. There were just too many people in one place, so the girls were told they could go play. Lily, Rosie, and the rest of the little girl cousins ran out to the barn and climbed up into the loft. It would be fun to sit at the open loft door and watch the huge crowd of people who were gathering at the farm. Papa said there might be as many as one thousand people coming through the farm today. The auctioneer walked around the farm and spoke in a loud, fast, rat-a-tat voice. Crowds of people followed him along the line of farm machinery that stood at the edge of the hayfield. Long lines of people snaked by the food stand, buying fresh homemade doughnuts and lemonade.

Lily enjoyed sitting and talking with her cousins as they watched all the activity. Her cousins were much more interesting than Effie Kauffman, who talked only about Aaron Yoder and Harvey Hershberger. Her cousins talked about books and games and horses.

Rosie dangled her legs over the edge of the loft, but Lily stayed back inside. She didn't want to risk falling out. The hayloft looked eerie. It was empty, swept clean. All the hay bales had been stacked on wagons to be sold at the auction.

The auction lasted until late afternoon. Lily watched as people loaded cows on trailers to take them to their new homes. She felt sorry for the cows and wondered if they felt sad that they had to leave their cow friends. She knew how it felt to say goodbye.

Today was another auction, but there would be no strangers at this auction—only Papa's brothers and sisters and their families. Today they would sell all of Grandpa Lapp's things and everything that Grandma Lapp no longer needed. Grandma was planning to keep only her bed, a dresser, her rocking chair, and a few of her favorite books and dishes.

Lily was amazed at how cheery Grandma seemed, even as most of her belongings were sold off. It was like a life was being washed away. "I'm so glad I'm doing this now," Grandma said. "It's nice to be able to see what my children want to have. If this waited until after I died, I would never know."

What a horrible thought! Lily didn't want Grandma to talk about dying. To not even think about it! Just the idea of it gave Lily the shivers.

Outside, church benches were set up as tables all over the yard. Mama, the aunts, and the older girl cousins helped clear out all the kitchen cupboards and organize things on the makeshift tables. Papa and the uncles were hard at work making ice cream—all different kinds of flavors. Lily's mouth watered at the thought of sampling every single flavor: strawberry, chocolate, butter pecan. The boy cousins pounded on large ice chunks to crush them into small enough pieces to fit into the ice-cream freezers. Lily, Rosie, and the other little girls couldn't decide where to be! Poring over all the items being offered for sale or watching the ice-cream making.

Grandma Lapp interrupted their discussion. "Would you girls like to be in charge of making lunch today? The women don't have time to make a big meal. If you'll make us plenty of sandwiches, that would suit nicely, especially with ice cream for dessert."

The girls followed Grandma Lapp into the kitchen where a dozen loaves of store-bought bread sat on the counter. On another counter were stacks of cheese, deli meat, and a big bowl of washed lettuce. "It's all yours, girls," Grandma said before she left to help move more things outdoors.

Rosie, the boss of the girl cousins but a nice one, decided to create an assembly line. Lily was at one end. She took two slices of bread, spread butter on them and handed them to Rosie, who spread salad dressing on top of the butter and passed them on. Cheese, meat, lettuce. By the end of the assembly, a huge pile of delicious-looking sandwiches had been created.

Lily and Rosie went outside to tell Grandma the sandwiches were ready. The ice cream had been finished, too. Everyone gathered in the yard for prayer, then took a sandwich or two before lining up to get ice cream. Lily followed Rosie to the row of ice cream freezers. Papa and the uncles were handing out scoops of ice cream as everyone walked by. Papa gave Lily a big scoop of strawberry ice cream, Uncle Ira gave her a big scoop of butter pecan, another uncle gave her a big scoop of chocolate, then peach, vanilla, cherry, blueberry, mixed berry, and finally, mint. Lily's plate was heavy with ice cream! How fun!

The girls sat on the grass in the shade of a big maple tree. Lily started eating. And eating. She couldn't decide which kind of ice cream was the best. Soon, she started to feel full. She ate slower and slower. So did her cousins. There were still huge scoops of melting ice cream left! How was she ever supposed to eat all of this?

Rosie put down her spoon and rubbed her tummy. "I can't eat one more bite."

"But what are we going to do with it?" Lily asked. They had all been taught to eat everything on their plate. Wasting food was a terrible thing.

Rosie looked around the yard. "Let's dump it in the outhouse."

The girls followed Rosie to the four-seater outhouse. They locked the door on the inside and scraped their plates down the holes. It was a shame, but what else could they do? When they were finished, they opened the door and stepped outside. There stood Grandma. She looked at the girls and their empty plates. Then she smiled. "Those uncles gave you all too much ice cream, didn't they?"

"Oh Grandma!" Lily said. "Don't be mad. We just couldn't eat another bite."

"Give the plates to me and I'll take them inside," Grandma said.

As Lily handed her empty plate to Grandma, she was so happy to think of her coming to live with them. Grandma might be old, but she understood children.

☙❧

Papa and Mama told Lily she could buy something today as a keepsake and remembrance of Grandpa and Grandma.

Lily's first thought was to buy a book. Her grandparents had rows and rows of books. But the next table held sets of pretty dishes. And the one after that had brightly colored fabrics.

As Lily wandered from table to table, the auction began. Uncle Ira was the auctioneer. He spoke slower than yesterday's professional auctioneer. For the first time she could actually understand what was getting sold! Uncle Ira started with the furniture, then the pretty dishes that Lily had been considering. Papa's sisters snatched those up. So far, everything had gotten much too expensive for Lily. Uncle Ira held up a book for everyone to see it. "Here's a favorite from our childhood," he said. "I'll pay thirty dollars for it. Anyone else care to make a bid?"

"Fifty!" Papa shouted.

Lily's hands flew to her mouth. What was Papa thinking?! To spend fifty dollars for one little book? Mama would not be happy with him.

But the bids kept on going. The price of that book went higher and higher. Everyone stopped to listen as the bidding continued. Two hundred dollars. Three hundred. Lily loved to read, but no book could be that interesting. And yet the price kept on rising! Four hundred dollars, four hundred twenty, four hundred twenty five, four hundred thirty. Going . . . going . . . gone! The book was sold to Uncle Ira for four hundred and thirty dollars. Another uncle called out, "Ira, you'd better read that book every day for the rest of your life to get your money's worth out of it."

Ira grinned, pleased, placed the book beside him, and went on to the next book. He held it up. "Can I get ten dollars?" No one said anything. "Can I get five?" Still no one spoke.

Lily looked at the money in her hand that Papa had given her. "I'll pay three dollars," she said.

"I have three dollars," Uncle Ira said. "Anyone want to bid four?"

Still, no one said anything. "Going . . . going . . . gone! Sold to Lily for three dollars."

Lily was so pleased! She had bought her first thing at an auction. Lily paid for her book as the auction continued. Papa bought a cuckoo clock that he remembered from his boyhood, Grandpa's hand drill, and an ugly chocolate brown and royal blue quilt. Mama whispered to her, "That quilt used to be on Papa's bed." When the auction was over, everyone gathered their things, said their goodbyes to Grandma, and started for home.

Everyone helped load the last of Grandma's things into a little trailer. Mr. Tanner's station wagon would haul the trailer back to Cloverdale with them. Lily was excited. It would be fun having Grandma living with them.

After a long drive, the Lapps arrived at Whispering Pines late at night. The boys were tucked into bed in their clothes. Grandma looked at the two rooms Papa had emptied for her. She shook her head. "It's too much for me. I don't need to take up so much room. You have a growing family. The sewing room will do just fine."

Grandma was adamant. So the next morning, Papa put the living room furniture back where it had been. Grandma's furniture was moved into the sewing room and she settled right in. Soon, it seemed like she had always been with them.

Dear Hannah,

Thank you for your letter telling me that Tom the hired boy is planning to get married soon. It's hard to believe that his fiancée is so terribly ugly. Maybe she has a wonderful personality?

So, Teacher Judith is not coming back next year. No one knows why, not even Effie (not really, though she made up lots of outlandish reasons so we would think she knew). My hunch is that it had to do with the fact that she never stuck around to listen to Mama's English lessons. She always had an errand to run.

I'm trying not to worry about who our new teacher will be, but I find it difficult not to worry about it. A teacher makes such a difference. Good teachers are so wonderful and bad teachers are so awful. Mama says to trust that God will provide just the teacher that Cloverdale needs.

You would hardly know Dannie had been so sick in May. Mama makes him take a long nap each afternoon, but most of the time he is as noisy and bothersome as he always was. It's wonderful.

Mama has been napping right along with Dannie—she said it's to encourage him to slow down and rest. While she is resting, Grandma Lapp is teaching me how to crochet. I have made so many white doilies this summer that Dannie said the living room looks like it's been covered with cobwebs.

Grandma Lapp is teaching me how to bake. I made a batch of popovers the other night, but they didn't pop like they were supposed to. Joseph called them popunders.

Mama is calling so I had better go. And yes, even though I enjoyed visiting my Lapp girl cousins in Kentucky, you will always be my most-favorite-of-all cousin.

Love,
Lily

Grandma's Stories

*E*arly on a June day, Lily helped Mama pick peas from the garden. She sat on the front porch swing beside Grandma Lapp to help her shell them for dinner. Joseph and Dannie tried to help but the peas flew all over the porch when they popped open the pods. More peas ended up on the porch floor than in the bowl, and soon Grandma shooed them away. Joseph took off to Papa's shop to work on a project, and Dannie went to play in the sandbox.

Lily opened another pod and carefully removed the little peas inside. She threw the empty husk into a five-gallon pail and started all over again. She sighed as she looked at all the peas left to be shelled. Three heaping bushel baskets full. "I think shelling peas is the most boring thing in the world," she said.

Grandma smiled. "I don't think anyone could ever say pea shelling is exciting, but it is relaxing. As for the most boring

job in the world, I think your papa might have an opinion about that."

"What's that?"

"Has he ever told you about the summer of cow watching?"

Lily brightened. A story was on its way! Grandma could spin wonderful yarns.

"Your papa was the youngest boy in the family. Boys run in the Lapp family, you know."

Oh, yes. Lily knew that.

"Daniel was always trying to keep up with his seven older brothers. Most of the time he would play with Menno, who was just a year older than him, but that didn't keep both of them from trying to tag along after the others. There came a summer that was especially hot. The cow pasture had been grazed until the grass was almost shorter than our mowed yard. Grandpa didn't want to start feeding hay until winter, but we knew we needed to do something to keep the livestock fed."

All the time Grandma was talking, she was shelling peas. Lily could talk or shell peas, but not both at the same time.

"Our neighbor had a field of clover right next to our pasture," Grandma continued. "He had retired from dairy farming and turned his farm into a hobby farm. He had a lot of different little animals like calves, rabbits, ducks, chickens, and a few horses. He didn't need all that land to raise crops. He had noticed we needed more grazing land for our cows, so he offered to let them graze on his field of clover. Grandpa went to look it over. The grass looked fine but the fence only went around three sides of the field.

"Grandpa decided to accept the neighbor's offer to graze the cows in his clover field. We waited to turn the cows out until after breakfast, and then he instructed the boys to station themselves along the edge of the field to watch the cows. If cows came too close to the edge of the field, their job was to chase them back. Grandpa figured that with eight boys, that should work. The cows could graze all day, and the boys could bring them home in the evening at milking time.

"Your papa was glad to be a part of the big boys' work. Day after day, the boys packed a lunch and took the cows out to the clover field. The cows were happy to have all that good green grass to eat and hardly ever tried to wander away.

"The boys whittled little wooden whistles and other toys,

but mostly, they sat and watched the cows. It wasn't too long before the boys grew bored with their job. And then one day, I was canning tomato juice when I saw Menno come running toward the house as fast as he could. I ran outside to see what was wrong. 'Molly stepped on Daniel's stomach!' he said."

Lily leaned forward in her chair. "What happened next?"

"I quickly ran to the field with Menno. He said that Daniel had fallen asleep in the tall grass under one of the trees and Molly didn't see him when she walked over to the shade to chew her cud. She stepped right on his stomach and wouldn't step off.

"When I got to your papa, he was still lying in the grass under a tree where he had fallen asleep, moaning and groaning like he was in terrible pain. Molly was a big old Brown Swiss cow and I was afraid with all that weight that she had torn something inside of your papa. I told Menno to run over to the neighbors to call an ambulance because I was afraid to move him. I was right, too, because when we got to the hospital the doctors wanted to do surgery right away to fix everything.

"Your papa spent the rest of the summer inside, in bed or on the couch. Folks brought him books, puzzles, and toys so he would have something to do while he recovered, but I know he would have rather been able to rejoin his brothers with cow watching."

Lily reached down for another pea. Why, the buckets were empty! They had shelled all of the peas while Grandma told the story of Papa and the summer of cow watching. She didn't mind doing a boring job when she could sit beside Grandma on the swing and listen to stories while they worked.

Lily finished sweeping the kitchen and hung the broom on the nail inside the broom closet. It was a rainy day and she was at loose ends. She wanted to do something today. Mama was helping Papa in the shop all day. Lily hurried to Grandma Lapp's room. She was sitting on her rocking chair crocheting an afghan. "Do you have any ideas for something to do today?"

Grandma dropped her hands in her lap, giving Lily's question some thought. "Would you like to try to bake a pie?"

That sounded like fun! Lily knew how to bake cake and cookies, but baking a pie was much harder. She had never tried to make a pie by herself.

Grandma put the yarn in the basket by her rocking chair. "Your papa had a favorite pie when he was a little boy. Let's go make it. I'll help you make the pie dough and roll it out."

In the kitchen, Grandma told Lily just what to do. She carefully measured out three cups of flour and ran a knife along the top of the measuring cup to scrape off any extra flour. She measured one cup of butter, cut it into the flour, and mixed it in with her hands. She mixed and mixed until all the crumbs looked the same size, the size of a pea, then she mixed some more. After adding the water she mixed and mixed and mixed. This was going to be the best mixed pie dough there ever was.

Grandma had gone upstairs to see if Paul was still napping. When she came downstairs, she asked Lily what could be taking her so long. Grandma peered into the bowl at the lump of dough. She poked at it with her finger and it left an indentation. "I should have told you not to mix it more than absolutely necessary. Otherwise it gets stiff."

Grandma dusted a little flour on the countertop and tried

to roll out the dough. It kept tearing and cracking. Mama's pie dough was elastic. This dough didn't look like dough.

Finally, Grandma gave up. "We're getting nowhere fast," Grandma said. "Go toss this lump of dough over the fence and I'll start making a new batch."

Lily ran outside with the ball of dough and tossed it over the fence. Sure enough, Dozer appeared out of nowhere and ran off with it. When Lily got back to the house, Grandma had almost finished making the new batch of pie dough. This time when she tried to roll it out it behaved the way it was supposed to—easy to stretch and push and pull.

Grandma fit the dough into a pie pan and showed Lily how to use her thumb and forefinger to pinch and twist the dough along the edges of the pie pan. Grandma's fingers flew around her half of the pie pan. Lily's fingers felt thick and clumsy. She went slowly and carefully, but her side didn't look nearly as pretty and even as Grandma's.

"What was Papa's favorite pie when he was a little boy?" Lily asked.

"It's called Milk Pie," Grandma said. "It's very simple to make. Take one cup of brown sugar and three tablespoons of flour and mix it together."

Lily measured the sugar and flour into a little bowl and mixed it together with a fork. "Does it matter how long I mix this?" Piecrusts were trickier than she had expected. Who knew you shouldn't mix and mix?

"No, not for this," Grandma said, peering into the bowl. "I think it's done. Go ahead and spread it on top of the dough in the bottom of one of the pie pans."

Lily dumped the sugar and flour mixture into a pie pan and spread it out.

"Now go ahead and add a cup and a half of milk and a little splash of vanilla," Grandma said.

Lily measured in the milk and carefully tipped the bottle of vanilla to make sure there wouldn't be more than a little splash. Vanilla was costly. "Now what?"

"Carefully stir it around with your fingers," Grandma said. "And it will be ready to bake."

Lily opened the oven door and Grandma slid the pie carefully inside. "It bakes for an hour and a half. Plenty of time to clean up the dishes we used and leave the kitchen spic-and-span for your mother."

That seemed like an awfully long time to wait for a pie. She couldn't wait to see Papa's face when she served him Milk Pie.

As soon as supper was over, Lily set the Milk Pie in front of Papa. His dark eyebrows shot up. "Why, it looks delicious!" He had two slices and cleaned up the last crumb from his plate. "Just like I remembered it as a boy."

If Lily were honest, she would have to say she thought it was a very boring pie. She wondered why this pie had been Papa's favorite. The only good thing she could think about it was that it was very easy to make, as long as Grandma made the tricky piecrust.

Papa's Flight

*L*ily and Mama were spading the flower bed in front of the house to plant rows of petunias and impatiens. Grandma sat on a chair with trays of flowers on her lap from the local greenhouse. She pulled one flower plant at a time from the container and handed it to Paul. Paul carried it slowly and carefully to Mama.

When the last impatien had been planted, Lily brushed dirt from her hands and stood back to look at the flower bed. It wouldn't be long before the plants filled in and covered the entire area with brightly colored flower petals.

Mama had a satisfied look on her face. "Lily, please water the flowers while I go prepare lunch." Grandma held Paul's hand to follow Mama into the house. As Lily filled the watering can with water from the hose, she watched Grandma and Paul walk slowly up the porch steps. It must be nice for Paul to have someone who walked at the same speed as he did.

Lily turned off the hose and picked up the watering can. She heard a noise and glanced back to discover Dozer had already dug holes in the flower bed. Mama's little pink impatiens lay on the ground, sad and broken. "Dozer!" Lily dropped the watering can and ran toward him. "Shoo, shoo, get out of here you naughty dog." She flapped her apron at him, but he darted away. Lily picked up the broken plants and replanted them. The flower bed didn't look nearly as good as it did when Mama had finished it. She hoped they would still grow big.

She glared at Dozer as she went inside the house for lunch. "I wish there was a way to teach Dozer to behave," she told Mama. "He dug holes in the flower bed."

Grandma was sitting in her rocking chair with Paul on her

lap, reading him a story. She looked up at Lily with a twinkle in her eye. "You should try flying at him."

Poor Grandma. She must be a little sun touched. "But Grandma, I can't fly," Lily said in her gentlest voice.

"Your papa flew at some dogs once," Grandma said. "Or maybe diving would be a better way to describe it."

Lily sat right down by Grandma's feet. A story was coming!

"We used to take eggs to sell in town every week when your papa was a boy. It was the boys' job to deliver the eggs. Ira or one of the older boys would drive the horse and your Papa liked to ride along." Joseph and Dannie appeared out of nowhere and sat by Grandma's rocking chair.

"There was one farm on the way to town that they didn't like to pass. Three big German shepherd dogs would race down the lane and bark at them. They'd even jump at the horse. The horse hated going by that farm, too. It was getting to be a problem." Grandma leaned forward on the rocking chair.

"So one day, as the boys were taking another load of eggs to town, they decided to teach those dogs a lesson they wouldn't forget. As they neared the farm, your papa stood on the back of the spring wagon with the horse's tie rope. When the dogs got close enough, he would swing it at them and chase them away.

"What happened next?" Joseph said.

"Yeah! What happened next?" Dannie echoed.

"As usual, the dogs came barreling up the lane, barking up a storm. Your papa swung the tie rope and the clip happened to hit the springs on the bottom of the wagon. It sounded like a gun had gone off. That was the last straw for the horse. He jumped and threw your papa off the back of the spring wagon, head first, right at the dogs. They hadn't expected a boy to come flying through the air toward them. Those dogs turned and ran home as fast as they could go."

"Was Papa hurt?" Lily asked.

"Your papa picked himself up and brushed himself off. He had quite a few cuts and bruises from his dive off the wagon. Ira stopped the horse and waited for your papa to hobble to the wagon and climb back in before they went on their way."

"But that," Grandma said with a smile in her voice, "was the last time those dogs tried to chase anyone."

The Train Tunnel

*E*arly one summer morning, Lily was surprised to find Papa in the kitchen making breakfast and Aunt Susie sitting at the table, inspecting burnt toast and lumpy porridge. Aunt Susie held a piece of toast in the air and frowned. "Daniel," she said in her slow, thick way, "I don't think this is right. Toast shouldn't be black."

"It's just a little overdone," Papa said. "Your stomach won't know the difference."

"Where's Mama?" Lily asked, rubbing her eyes.

Joseph and Dannie tumbled downstairs and into the kitchen. They stopped abruptly at the sight of Papa in the kitchen.

"She's still upstairs," Papa said, putting a container of milk on the table.

Aunt Susie took a tiny bite of the blackened toast and spit it out. "I don't think I can eat charcoal toast."

"Is Mama sick?" Lily asked.

246

Aunt Susie's eyes went wide. "Daniel, is my sister Rachel sick?" Her eyebrows knit together in a worried look.

"Rachel is fine, Susie," Papa said. "Just fine. Grandma Lapp and Grandma Miller are with her. They're . . . having a long talk." He wiped his forehead with his shirtsleeve. "It's already warm. It's going to be a hot day today." He looked out the window at the rising sun, peeking through the tops of the trees.

Lily took a bite of lumpy porridge. She never liked porridge, but this tasted like glue. She put down her spoon. Her appetite was gone. Everything felt strange. Why was Papa cooking? Why would Lily's grandmothers be upstairs having a long talk with Mama on a warm summer morning? Long talks with her grandmothers weren't unusual—Papa often said both of them were blessed with a gift of gab—but the long talks took place on the porch or in the living room, after the day's work was done.

Papa turned to Lily. "After Paul wakes up, I want you to take Aunt Susie and your brothers out for a few hours. Maybe a picnic. Anyplace you'd like."

Lily and Aunt Susie exchanged a happy look. "Can we make the picnic?" Lily said.

The pot with the awful porridge started to bubble over on the stovetop so Papa hurried over to turn off the burner. "Yes. As soon as breakfast is over, you can prepare a picnic."

At the exact same time, Lily and Aunt Susie said, "Breakfast is done!" The boys looked up in surprise. They didn't mind eating lumpy porridge and burnt toast. Sometimes, Lily thought they didn't have any taste buds at all. They ate anything that was in front of them.

A mournful moo floated in from the barn. Papa wiped his hands on a rag. "Pansy needs milking. Lily, I'm counting on you to handle everything in the kitchen." He stopped at the door. "Everyone stay downstairs. Give Mama some privacy."

As soon as the door closed behind Papa, Lily turned to Joseph. "Where should we go?"

"I want to go out to Teaskoota's. I promised him I'd show him my rock collection."

Lily rolled her eyes. Joseph and his rocks. Who'd want to look at rocks, anyway? But she liked the idea of visiting their kind old friend. It would be cooler in the mountains and they could share their picnic with him. "Aunt Susie, let's get the picnic ready before Paul wakes up."

Lily and Aunt Susie packed Mama's chocolate chip cookies, shoo-fly tarts, half of a blueberry pie—and then remembered sandwiches. They slapped slices of bread with peanut butter and strawberry jam. Just as Lily put it all in a basket, she heard Paul calling from his crib. She hurried to get him and change his clothes. On the way back down the stairs, she stopped to listen beside Mama's door. All she could hear were the sweet low voices of her grandmothers, chatting away. She didn't hear Mama's voice at all, but the grandmothers sounded cheerful. She heard the squeak of a rocking chair as someone rose to her feet, so Lily hurried down the stairs with Paul. She didn't want to be caught eavesdropping. She did eavesdrop—often—but she certainly didn't want to be caught. She still thought it was odd that Mama and the grandmothers chose early morning for a visit, but she was too excited for the day's adventure to think any more about it.

❧

Joseph and Dannie ran up the trail while Aunt Susie and Lily took turns carrying Paul and the picnic basket. Joseph had insisted on bringing Dozer despite Lily's objections. Dozer was nothing but a nuisance. He never obeyed anybody except Papa.

Lily worried it might be too far to hike all the way to Teaskoota's log cabin on such a hot day. On the other hand, the cool, dark air of the tunnel would feel good. It took even longer because Paul kept wanting to get down and walk. Finally, they reached the tunnel and Dozer disappeared inside. At first, Aunt Susie didn't want to go in. "It's too dark," she said.

"Give your eyes a moment or two to adjust," Lily told her. "Just stay on the tracks and we'll be out the other end in no time. You'll like how cool the air feels."

Aunt Susie followed Lily in, tentatively, until a sweet cool breeze floated around her. She smiled and picked Paul up. "Hold on tight to me, Paul." Her confidence grew as they ventured farther into the tunnel. "I wish we could have our picnic in here."

"It'll be cooler at Teaskoota's log cabin," Joseph said. "At least cooler than back at the house."

Water dripped down the sides of the tunnel as they trudged along. Then they heard a funny sound up ahead and Dozer started to bark furiously. The hair on Lily's neck stood up. Something seemed strange. Eerie.

Lily reached out to stop Joseph from going any farther, but when she stepped out, she slipped in a puddle of wet gravel and her ankle twisted, jamming under the metal railing. She felt a shooting pain. Joseph tried to help her up, but her foot was tightly pinned. Dozer was up ahead, barking like a crazy dog, and then Paul started to wail. Aunt Susie contributed a scream. Lily had to think fast. She was frantic, but sometimes her best ideas came when she was in such a state.

"Joseph, take Aunt Susie and the boys and go get Papa to come help."

"It might be faster if I run up the tunnel to Teaskoota's," Joseph said.

Whatever Dozer was barking at was a worry to Lily. If it happened to be a snake, Aunt Susie would scream. "I think you need to go back to the house—"

"But—"

"Go, Joseph!" Lily's foot hurt badly. She tried not to cry. If she cried, Aunt Susie would start to howl.

"Do you want Dannie to stay here with you?"

Lily looked at Dannie, who was starting to wander up toward Dozer. He didn't mind Lily at all, and he was still weak from the appendix surgery. "No. He can help Aunt Susie with Paul."

Joseph looked all around. "Where's the picnic basket?"

Lily's ankle was throbbing. Who cared about lunch at a time like this? "Joseph, GO!"

Joseph grabbed Dannie's hand and helped Aunt Susie pick up Paul to walk back out of the tunnel. Lily watched until they had disappeared. She tried to gently pull her foot out from under the railing, but each time she pulled, splinters from the rotten railroad ties pricked her foot. Tears started rolling down her face. She didn't want to be left alone in a dark tunnel with only crazy Dozer for company. She called to him and he ran back to her, then licked her face. He stiffened and she figured he was going to leave her to run after Joseph. Suddenly, Dozer flew down the tunnel again, barking and growling. Lily saw a big shadow move, way down in the dark. Then an ear-piercing growl, so loud it could have raised the hair on the dead, filled the tunnel.

A bear!

❦

Lily heard Dozer's awful snarls and the bear's ferocious growls, and she thought she was surely going to die. She tried to dig the gravel under the metal railing that pinned her foot. Suddenly, someone came up behind her and started to scoop gravel away with his hands. She looked up, confused. She was sure Papa had come, but it was Aaron Yoder.

Carefully, Aaron eased her foot out from under the railing. Her foot was free! "Can you walk on it, Lily?"

"I'll try. There's a bear down there. He's fighting Dozer."

"I warned you not to go in this tunnel. I told you about the bear and her cubs."

And wasn't that just like Aaron? He thought *now* was the time to give her a lecture? She tried to stand up but couldn't put weight on her sore ankle. Terrible sounds came from down the tunnel, where the bear and Dozer were fighting.

Aaron looked down the tunnel. "We need to get out of here. Lily, put your arms around my neck."

"Never."

"Now!" He swept her up in his arms and ran down the tunnel. As soon as they were out in the daylight, Aaron set Lily down on a tree stump. Out of nowhere, Harvey Hershberger ran over to them.

Harvey peered at Lily's swollen ankle. "Oh, that's broke, for sure."

It was twice the size of her other foot, bleeding and scraped up. "Where did the two of you come from?" she asked.

"We were heading out to the fishing hole when we bumped into Joseph," Harvey said. "He told us you needed help, so we came straight away."

Aaron gave Harvey a sharp look.

"I acted as lookout," Harvey said.

Aaron rolled his eyes.

A sharp bark from the tunnel drew their attention. "Dozer!" Lily tried to climb off the tree stump. "I've got to call him out."

Aaron had his hands on his hips, staring at the tunnel. "Harvey, you go get him."

Harvey's eyes went wide as half dollars. "Oh no. Not me. I don't like tunnels so much. Or bears. I'll get Lily home while you fetch the dog."

Aaron threw Harvey a disgusted look and started toward the tunnel.

"Aaron!" Lily said. "Don't go back in. Just call to Dozer. Whistle for him. But don't go back in."

Naturally, Aaron paid her no mind. He picked up a big stick and walked tentatively into the tunnel, calling and whistling for Dozer.

"Aaron'll be fine," Harvey said, waving off any worries. "He's a bright boy. But I'd better get you home so your mother can see to your ankle." He scooped her up in his arms.

Once again, Lily found herself picked up and carried off by another boy. Twice in one day. *Humiliating!* If her ankle weren't throbbing like it was, she would be furious. Those boys acted like she was a bag of flour.

Just as they reached the road, they saw Papa running toward them. "Lily, what happened to you?" He examined her swollen ankle and took her from Harvey. "Thank you, Harvey. Thank you for your help."

"No problem at all," Harvey said, quite pleased with himself. "I was in the right place at the right time. That's just the kind of fellow I am."

Aaron Yoder came jogging down the trail, a bothered look on his face.

252

"Did you get Dozer?" Lily said.

Aaron shook his head and looked away. "No."

Papa thanked both boys and started for home. On the way, Lily told him about the bear and about Dozer. New concern flooded Papa's face.

"If only Dozer would have learned to listen!" she said. She dreaded telling Joseph that Dozer was gone. From the serious look on Aaron's face, she thought Dozer might have been killed by the bear.

"Lily," Papa said gently, "don't you realize that Dozer was protecting you from the bear? He was trying to keep the bear from getting close to you. Just the way a mother bird tries to coax a threat away from the nest."

What? She had assumed Dozer had tangled with the bear because he was just being dumb Dozer. She had never liked Dozer, had never wanted to play with him, had never forgiven him for chewing up Sally . . . but here he had saved her life. One tear started, then another.

"Don't cry, Lily. Your ankle doesn't look broken, just a bad sprain. It will mend quickly and we still have Joseph's crutches from last summer. Don't cry."

But that was the problem with crying. Once she started, she couldn't stop. Her ankle hurt, her sadness over Dozer hurt, and so did her pride. To have to be rescued by Aaron Yoder and Harvey Hershberger was just about the worst thing that could have happened to her. She should be grateful—who knew what might have happened before Papa arrived? But those boys would brag about the rescue all summer long. She would never live it down.

Aunt Susie was out on the porch when Papa carried Lily up the steps. She had already forgotten about Lily's fall in the tunnel. Her face was lit up with happiness. "Lily, there's a surprise! Two surprises!"

"First things first, Susie," Papa said. "I want to make sure Lily's ankle is taken care of. Then she can see the surprise."

Papa set Lily on a chair in the kitchen. Grandma Miller and Grandma Lapp fussed over her, examining the ankle and wiping her tears away. Gently, Papa cleaned the bad scrapes, washed off the blood, and took out splinters with tweezers. He turned Lily's ankle, holding it carefully, until he was convinced it wasn't broken and the grandmothers agreed. "Just a bad sprain. But let's get cold water on it." Papa wrapped Lily's ankle with a cold, wet rag.

"Can she see the surprises now?" Aunt Susie asked, clasping her hands together in excitement.

Papa laughed. "I'll have to carry you upstairs, Lily, to see the surprises." He picked Lily up and took her into Mama's room. Mama was lying in bed. In each of her arms lay a tiny, red, wrinkled baby. Why, Effie had actually been right about something! Mama *was* going to have a baby. Two babies! Lily was finally getting a sister. *Two* sisters!

"Oh, Mama, can I name them?"

But Mama's eyes were fixed on Lily's wrapped-up foot. "What happened to you?"

"It's a long story," Papa said, cutting Lily off just as she was about to launch into the bear story.

Dannie came into the room and sidled next to Mama to look at the babies.

"Lily's ankle isn't broken, Rachel," Papa said. "We can tell Mama all about your adventure later. She needs to rest now."

He turned to go, but Lily leaned over his shoulder. "Mama, can I name my sisters?"

Papa froze. Slowly, he turned around so Lily was facing Mama and the babies. He and Mama exchanged a look. "Lily," Papa said in his gentlest voice, "these little babies . . . they're . . . not . . ."

"Oh no," Lily said, as a thought started to dawn. "No, no, no." A horrible feeling started in the bottom of her stomach.

Dannie smiled at Lily. His grown-up front teeth were about halfway in now, and he didn't whistle and spit quite so much when he talked. "They're brothers!"

A Very Mad Bull

Twin babies, Lily thought, were much, much more trouble than just two babies. One or the other was always crying, eating, or needing a diaper change. Both grandmothers were now at Whispering Pines to help, which was the only nice thing about having twin babies.

Papa and Mama named the babies after Grandpa Lapp: Phineas and Enos. Lily loved her grandfather, but what horrible names to give two little funny-looking boys!

She still hadn't gotten over her disappointment that they weren't the sisters Effie had predicted. There were so many boys in this house. Lily tried to show interest in the babies, for Mama's sake, but it wasn't very sincere.

Mama thought they were beautiful boys, and Lily didn't want to hurt her feelings with the truth. They were odd-looking babies: bald and toothless, with ears that were too big for their heads. Dannie and Paul had been ugly babies, and they looked pretty normal now, so she hoped these new babies' looks might improve in time. She couldn't remember Joseph as a baby, but she suspected he had been ugly, too.

Mostly, Lily tried to stay outdoors with Dannie and Joseph, even on crutches with a sprained ankle, so she wouldn't be called on to rock a crying baby. She was trying to do all she could to keep Joseph from thinking about Dozer. When she had told Joseph that the bear might have killed Dozer, he covered his hands with his ears and refused to believe it. He was adamant about it, convinced Dozer had fought off the bear. He was always on the lookout for that dog and wanted to go search for him in the train tunnel, but Papa wouldn't let him. The train tunnel was off limits this summer.

Every time Lily thought about Dozer, she felt a stone drop in her stomach. She was grieving over that silly, crazy, pest of a dog.

On Saturday morning, babies or not, it was housecleaning day. The grandmothers told Joseph and Dannie to carry every rug in the house out to the front porch. It was Lily's job to shake the rugs, which wasn't easy with a sprained ankle. She picked up a dark blue rug from the pile of rugs. Six hard shakes on one end, then she flipped it over the porch railing and gave the other end six shakes. Good enough. She rolled it up and reached for the next one. She didn't like the little bits of dirt that flew off and stung her face and arms. Shaking rugs and washing dishes topped the list of things Lily didn't like to do but had to do quite often. These rugs needed to be whacked every single Saturday.

If anyone was to ask Lily's opinion, she would get rid of the rugs. There were too many rugs in the house. One for each door. One in front of the kitchen sink and another in front of the stove. Two for each bedroom, and one for each rocking chair and in front of the sofa. It might not seem like all that much until they sat on a pile waiting for Lily to shake the dirt off of them.

As she rolled up the last rug, she made up her mind to ask Mama if she could have the afternoon to play. Maybe she would take Joseph and Dannie for a walk in the woods or gather some buttercups in the pasture. She could get around pretty easily on the crutches. And wouldn't Mama like a bouquet of buttercups?

"Yes, you can all go play," Mama said when Lily popped into her room to ask. She peeked at the babies in their cradles and was glad they were both sound asleep. One squeaked while he slept. She thought that was Phineas, but she still couldn't tell one twin from the other.

Lily went to the shop to find Joseph and Dannie. They were happy to go along with her.

"Let's pretend we're playing pioneers," Joseph said. "We could go to the top of Mr. Beal's hill and then pretend we're going to California by covered wagon. We can pretend our house is in California."

Mr. Beal was very nice about letting Lily and Joseph walk through his fields. She shielded her eyes against the sun and scanned the fields, but she didn't see Mr. Beal working anywhere. "Okay. But go slowly. Crutches are hard in the field."

"What will we use for covered wagons?" Dannie asked.

"People used to walk beside their wagons," Joseph said. "I know that for a fact. So we can pretend to be walking beside a covered wagon."

They walked across the pasture and slipped through the fence to reach Mr. Beal's hayfield. Just last week, Mr. Beal had baled hay, so the grass was nice and short except for a few clumps that the mower had missed, which made it easier for Lily. They crossed the hayfield and walked through the cornfield. She did not like walking through cornfields. Even though the corn was only up to her knees, the long green leaves brushed and scratched against her as she walked. Cuts from corn leaves felt just like paper cuts. Plus, there was always the worry of snakes.

She was glad when they got to the other side and climbed the hill. When they reached the top, they were out of breath and sat down to rest. She rubbed her ankle. It was a little sore, a little stiff, but not too bad.

Joseph jumped up. "Time to head out," he said in his imitation of a grown-up voice. "I'm the leader of the wagon train so everyone has to follow me."

Lily put Dannie behind Joseph. He could be hard to keep track of if he wasn't following Joseph around. They walked slowly down the hill and made their way back through the cornfield. When they came out on the other side, Joseph cupped his hands around his mouth and hollered, "Buffalo ahead!"

Mr. Beal's cows were grazing in the hayfield. As the children started across the field, it was fun to pretend the lazy cows were buffalo. Halfway through, a cow lifted her head and looked at them. "Moo!"

Lily thought possibly, just possibly, that small young cow was Nelly, the princess calf Papa had given to Mr. Beal. Then the cow started walking toward them. "Moo!" Several more joined in. "Moo! Moo!"

This felt strange. Cows didn't usually care what went on around them as long as there was grass to eat. More and more cows started to walk toward them. They walked faster. The moos grew louder as more and more cows joined in the chorus.

And then Lily's heart almost stopped.

Right in front of them was Mr. Beal's enormous black bull, and he didn't look happy. He walked a few steps toward them and then stopped and pawed the ground and snorted angrily.

"We'd better get out of here," Lily said as calmly as she could. Joseph grabbed Dannie's hand and they hurried as fast as they could, Lily hobbling behind on crutches. Lily could hear the bull's snorts getting louder, but she didn't dare look back.

"Run, Joseph! Take Dannie and go!" she screamed. Then she stumbled over a clump of grass and her ankle twisted again. She fell flat on her face. Joseph and Dannie kept on running while Lily tried to scramble back to her feet. Forget the crutches! Desperate, she hopped on one foot as fast as she could. Joseph and Dannie had made it to the fence. "Run, Lily, run! The bull is running at you!"

Lily felt as if she were stuck in a bad dream, as if she were running in quicksand. She tried to run without putting much weight on her weak ankle, but she couldn't move fast enough.

A strange sound started across the pasture, then got louder and louder. A bark. A familiar bark.

"Dozer!" Joseph yelled. "It's Dozer! I knew he'd come home!"

Dozer raced toward Lily, then ran past her, headfirst at the bull, then around its back to snap at its heels. The bull spun around in a circle, and Dozer kept nipping at him, running off, then stopping and snapping. Over and over, until that bull had moved far, far away from Lily.

She reached the fence and rolled under it to safety on the

other side. She lay there panting and gasping for breath. When she finally opened her eyes, she saw Aaron Yoder and Harvey Hershberger, of all people, staring down at her.

"Did she die from fright?" Harvey asked.

"Naw, I don't think so," Aaron said. He had Lily's crutches in his hand.

Lily sat right up, just in time for Dozer to jump through the fence and onto her lap, covering her face with licks. "Oh, Dozer! Where did you come from?" Dozer was beside himself. His whole body was wiggling. His tail wagged so fast and so hard, Lily thought it might whirl right off. He ran from Lily to Joseph to Dannie and back to Lily.

"I found him down by the fishing hole," Harvey said.

Aaron looked at him as if he'd lost his mind. "*You* found him?"

Harvey shrugged. "I helped."

Aaron rolled his eyes. "He's a little beat up from the bear, but no bones are broke. I thought you'd want to see him so I brought him right over."

Lily gave Dozer a closer look—he had some scrapes that were healing, and one ear looked a little torn, but he was the same old Dozer. Wonderful and exasperating.

The bull glared at them, snorting and pawing the ground. "Let's go home, Dannie," Joseph said. "Come on, Dozer!" The two boys started off across the yard.

But Dozer wouldn't budge. He was waiting for Lily.

"That bull is gonna come right through the fence if we don't get out of here," Aaron said. He held out a hand to help Lily to her feet. Harvey immediately held out his hand to her, too.

Lily looked at both of their hands, reluctant to take them. It wasn't so long ago that Aaron had tried to help her up on the school yard and then released her so she fell back down again. She couldn't quite get past her suspicion about the motives of Aaron Yoder. She was doubly suspicious of Harvey Hershberger.

But then the bull started to ram the fence with his big head. Lily grabbed the boys' hands and they practically lifted her into the air. Aaron handed the crutches to her and the three of them started off toward Whispering Pines, Lily limping between the boys.

When Lily realized Dozer wasn't following, she stopped and turned back. "Come on, Dozer! Let's go home!" Dozer gave a few more warning barks to the bull, then turned and followed behind Lily, Harvey, and Aaron to the safety of home.

After all, he was a fine dog, Dozer was.

Questions about the Amish

Why didn't Grandma Lapp go live in a retirement home, like most people do, instead of moving into Lily's crowded house? Family is very important to the Amish, and the elderly are treated with great respect. The Amish don't have retirement homes. They don't have nursing homes, either. Instead, the elderly are kept at home and family members share caregiving. They consider such caregiving to be an opportunity to give back to the parent or grandparent who has given so much to them. Many Amish farms have a grandfather's house, called a *Grossdaadi Haus*, so that grandparents can live nearby but have a separate entrance and kitchen.

What is an Amish church service like? The Amish hold their twice-a-month church service in homes. Every church family takes a turn hosting church, usually once a year. Homes are built or adjusted with large doors to open the interior to accommodate a large gathering for such a service. The Amish worship service lasts three or more hours. Females sit on one side, males on the other. From the very start, children are trained to remain quiet during the service, though often a plate of cookies or pretzels will be handed down the line of benches. After the church service, they share a simple meal together. The afternoon is reserved for visits with neighbors and friends.

Do the Amish have music in church? Music sung at church is entirely a cappella, without instruments, because that would be considered showy. There is no harmony so that no individual stands out. "We all sing in one voice, in unison," said an Amish dairy farmer. The congregation sings from the *Ausbund*—a term meaning "selection" or "anthology"—a hymnal with only printed words. Tunes, learned by memory and passed down through the centuries, are sung not with many voices but with one. The slow tunes, or *langsam Weis*, as the Amish call them, were composed by martyrs in prison.

Every Amish church service begins and ends with a hymn. Some of the hymns can take as long as twenty minutes to sing. For three hundred years the Amish have sung these hymns in just this way, and so it will always be.

What is an Ordnung? Ordnung is a Pennsylvania Dutch word. Because the Amish have no centralized church government, each local church maintains its own set of guidelines, or Ordnung. While many core values are shared, there is a great deal of variation in Ordnung from church to church.

How do the Amish choose their church leaders? A typical Amish church has a bishop, two ministers, and a deacon. Those leaders are chosen through a divine lottery. The only way to become a minister is to be "hit" by the "casting of the lot," just the way Judas Iscariot's replacement was made in the book of Acts. Nominations for the position are whispered to the existing minister from the members, including women, though only married men can be nominated. It's a system to ensure that a person of good reputation will become a leader. Whoever receives more than three votes is nominated. Then a slip of paper with "You are the one" written on it is put in an *Ausbund*—the Amish hymnal. The same number of hymnals as there are nominees are placed on a bench in front of the congregation. Only one hymnal holds the slip of paper. With a divine nod, the man who picks the hymnal with the lot inside becomes the selected minister. When the need for a bishop arises, he will be chosen from the ministers, just the way it happened with Lily's uncle Jacob.

Why did Uncle Jacob seem sad to be chosen as a bishop? Amish ministers, bishops, and deacons serve without pay and without formal training. They must spend long hours in preparation for the Sunday service and take on the burden of caring for the church members, the way a shepherd cares for his flock of sheep. All that extra work and worry, on top of their own families and jobs. Uncle Jacob's response was very typical—he felt the weight and responsibility of this new role on his shoulders.

Mary Ann Kinsinger was raised Old Order Amish in Somerset County, Pennsylvania. She met and married her husband, whom she knew from school days, and started a family. After they chose to leave the Amish church, Mary Ann began a blog, *A Joyful Chaos*, as a way to capture her warm memories of her childhood for her own children. From the start, this blog found a ready audience and even captured the attention of key media players, such as the influential blog *AmishAmerica* and the *New York Times*. She lives in Pennsylvania.

Suzanne Woods Fisher's grandfather was one of eleven children, raised Old Order German Baptist, in Franklin County, Pennsylvania. Suzanne has many, many, *many* wonderful Plain relatives. She has written bestselling fiction and nonfiction books about the Amish and couldn't be happier to share Mary Ann's stories with children. When Suzanne isn't writing, she is raising puppies for Guide Dogs for the Blind. She lives in California with her husband and children and Tess and Toffee, her big white dogs.

DON'T MISS THE STONEY RIDGE SEASONS SERIES!

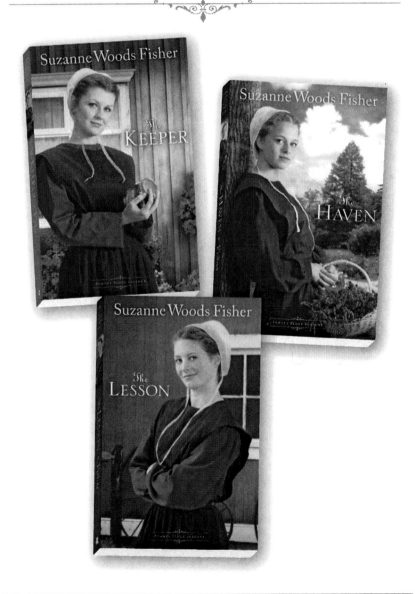

WELCOME TO A PLACE OF UNCONDITIONAL LOVE AND UNEXPECTED BLESSINGS

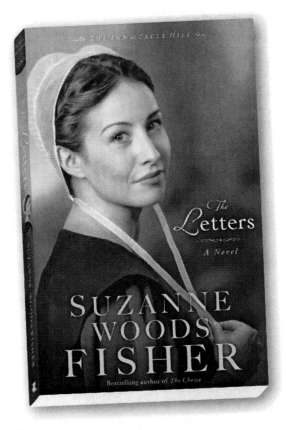

Rose Schrock is a simple woman with a simple plan. Determined to find a way to support her family and pay off her late husband's debts, she sets to work to convert part of her Amish farmhouse into an inn. As Rose finalizes preparations for visitors, she prays, asking God to bless each guest who comes to stay. She could never imagine the changes that await her own family—and her heart—at the Inn at Eagle Hill.

Revell
a division of Baker Publishing Group
www.RevellBooks.com

Available Wherever Books Are Sold
Also Available in Ebook Format

Longing for a simpler life? Hoping to slow down and catch a breath in the midst of a busy day?

The *Amish Wisdom* Mobile App helps you do just that . . . and more. It provides you with a daily proverb, drawn from the Pennsylvania Dutch tradition, to bring a moment of peace to your day. And you can also listen to Suzanne Woods Fisher's *Amish Wisdom* radio program.

Be the First to Hear about Other New Books from REVELL!

Sign up for announcements about new and upcoming titles at

RevellBooks.com/SignUp

Don't miss out on our great reads!

CPSIA information can be obtained at www.ICGtesting.com
Printed in the USA
LVOW10s1624250315

431990LV00002B/296/P

9 780800 721350